S0-AGZ-717

"You really don't know who I am, do you?"

The luminous green eyes searched Helen's face. What an undeniably attractive man this mysterious Scot was, she thought, but he left her utterly cold.

"No," she said. "I have no idea who you are. And I'm not interested."

"Fine." He smiled. "It's settled, then. We share the villa, and we don't intrude on each other's privacy, and you regard me as nothing more than a temporary friend."

"That's all you can expect to be," Helen said, rising abruptly. "You see, Mr.—, I've come to the conclusion I don't like you very much."

He turned so he could look at her.

"I can understand that," he said without amusement. "Because I don't like me, either, my dear. Not one little bit."

These books may be available at your local bookseller.

For a list of all titles currently available,
send your name and address to:

Harlequin Reader Service
P.O. Box 52040, Phoenix, AZ 85072-2040
Canadian address: P.O. Box 2800, Postal Station A,
5170 Yonge St., Willowdale, Ont. M2N 5T5

CLAUDIA JAMESON

dawn of a new day

Harlequin Books

TORONTO • NEW YORK • LONDON
AMSTERDAM • PARIS • SYDNEY • HAMBURG
STOCKHOLM • ATHENS • TOKYO • MILAN

For Lyn,
who saw it coming...

———————————————

Harlequin Presents first edition November 1984
ISBN 0-373-10737-4

Original hardcover edition published in 1984
by Mills & Boon Limited

Copyright © 1984 by Claudia Jameson. All rights reserved.
Philippine copyright 1984. Australian copyright 1984.
Except for use in any review, the reproduction or utilization of
this work in whole or in part in any form by any electronic,
mechanical or other means, now known or hereafter invented,
including xerography, photocopying and recording, or in any
information storage or retrieval system, is forbidden without
the permission of the publisher, Harlequin Enterprises Limited,
225 Duncan Mill Road, Don Mills, Ontario, Canada M3B 3K9.

All the characters in this book have no existence outside the
imagination of the author and have no relation whatsoever to
anyone bearing the same name or names. They are not even
distantly inspired by any individual known or unknown to the
author, and all the incidents are pure invention.

The Harlequin trademarks, consisting of the words
HARLEQUIN PRESENTS and the portrayal of a Harlequin,
are trademarks of Harlequin Enterprises Limited and are
registered in the Canada Trade Marks Office; the portrayal
of a Harlequin is registered in the United States Patent
and Trademark Office.

Printed in U.S.A.

CHAPTER ONE

HAD there been anyone else around, she would have felt idiotic sunbathing in a pair of knee-length socks and a bikini, but she was still wary of getting the sun on her legs, not knowing whether direct exposure to sunlight would cure or worsen the rash on her calves.

Helen Good spread out her gaily coloured beach towel, fished in her bag for her sunglasses and the paperback she had bought at Heathrow Airport, and tried yet again to become engrossed in the book. For the past five days she had been on Trinini Island, and each morning she had soaked up the sun and absorbed the silence on this beautiful private beach.

Two minutes later the book was discarded and she sat up, pushing down one of her socks so she could inspect the progress, or lack of it, as far as the rash was concerned.

'It's psychosomatic, Helen,' her doctor had told her when she had finally gone to him and poured out her troubles. Well, some of her troubles. 'It'll vanish in its own good time.'

At first she had refused to believe this, thinking it was an allergy to something or other, but there was no sign of it on any other part of her body. It was only on the inside of her calves, covering a few inches, a series of bumps and tiny circular welts beneath the surface of the skin. It didn't irritate, it didn't even look too bad, but it was *there*.

The cream that the doctor had prescribed had failed to help, so had the tablets he had given her on her second visit. And yes, he had been right, the root cause of it was psychosomatic. If she could sort out the turmoil in her mind, if she could come to terms with all that had happened, then she would be well on her way to a complete cure. She would start eating properly

7

again, she would start sleeping properly, without having nightmares, and she would have the courage to throw away the small brown bottle of tranquillisers which beckoned to her every time she saw them in her bag.

'Two lots of tablets?' She had looked questioningly at the prescription the doctor had given her, querying the second item. On learning that they were tranquillisers, she had protested, insisting that she would not take them.

'They'll help you to sleep, they'll help you to cope. Don't worry, it's only a temporary measure. There will be no repeat prescription, I can assure you of that.'

But Helen had resisted the temptation, afraid that she might become dependent on them—almost certain that she would. Still, she carried them around with her as a sort of . . . a sort of insurance.

So far, the bottle had remained unopened and, considering the trauma she had experienced last Friday, Helen congratulated herself for that, thinking it something of an achievement. It was true that Corinne Clayman had encouraged her to drink several glasses of brandy after last Friday's incident, and that Helen had not needed much encouragement, but that was nothing to worry about. Alcohol was something Helen could take or leave, without any fear of becoming addicted.

Last Friday, after the police had left, she had sat motionless for a long, long time. How long, she didn't know. She had sat perfectly still, staring yet seeing nothing, feeling as though she had been raped—a sort of spiritual rape. Getting home from work to find that her house had been burgled was horrible. It wasn't just the shock of it, the damage that had been done, the mindless destruction of things which were priceless to her but which could have no value to anyone else, the worst thing was the knowledge that someone had been through all her personal belongings. Even her bedding had been rooted through and thrown to the floor.

She got to her feet and walked to the water's edge, standing with her back to the sea so she could look at the sweep of white sand along the bay, the edge of the island and the gorgeous white villa which stood overlooking all this, the villa which was hers to use for as long as she wanted it.

Sanity was returning. After being here for five days she had started to think clearly again. She could not think too far back, but at least the events of the past week were not too painful to remember. That was progress, surely? With luck she might even be able to reach a decision about her future before this holiday was over. For the past four months the ability to make even the smallest decision had been beyond her. But then for the past four months she had been on the edge of a nervous breakdown. Her doctor had realised it, her boss had realised it, but it was only now that Helen could see it for herself.

She pulled off her socks and threw them on to the sand, wading into the water until it was waist-high. She swam around slowly on her back, enjoying the sheer satin luxury of water which was turquoise blue and incredibly clear. The privacy, the solitude, was blissful. The beauty, the tranquillity and peacefulness of the island was starting to communicate itself to her. And it was by sheer fluke that she was lucky enough to find herself here in the Bahamas.

The villa had been loaned to her by a stranger, a woman who had wanted to repay Helen for what she had considered a kindness—something Helen had considered a mere duty. But the woman had been insistent on returning that 'kindness', and Helen had been in no fit state to argue about it.

She was glad, now, that she had been unable to argue with the woman. This island was not far short of paradise, and there was little else to do here but think. Since she was still easily tired, she resumed her sunbathing after ten minutes or so, covering her straight black hair with a large-brimmed sun-hat and looking out to sea. In the distance, across the water, was Great Exuma Island, and in the foreground a flotilla of yachts floated by. She followed their progress, realising for the first time that she had seen dozens of yachts and boats since she had been here. Of course the surrounding cays were absolutely ideal for yachting, but for the first few days she had been in too much of a mental fog to appreciate what was going on around the island and the beauty of her surroundings. She had much exploring to do, if only she could summon up the energy ...

It was odd realising she had been here for almost a week. The days had slipped rapidly by, merging into one continuous stretch of time almost unbroken by sleep, yet she could remember starkly every single detail of last Friday from the moment she had woken in the morning.

As usual, she had woken feeling tired and unable to face the day. As usual, she had forced herself to go through the motions of getting to the art gallery where she worked. It was a long and inconvenient journey, entailing a bus ride from the village where she lived to Reading Station, a train to Paddington Station in London, then a bus ride to the art gallery in the West End. And all the way to work she had been thinking about handing in her notice, about finding a job nearer home, about selling the house. But, as usual, she had been unable to make a decision.

It was her boss, Geoffrey Mortimer, who had urged her to take some time off work, who had told her kindly but firmly that she was neither use nor ornament to him at the moment—though not quite in as many words. Things had come to a head shortly after lunch time, when Helen had been in the middle of telephoning an advertisement in to a national newspaper. Geoffrey Mortimer had walked into the office, taken the phone from her hand and finished the job himself.

'You were giving them the wrong dates, Helen. The exhibition is from the tenth to the twenty-ninth.' Geoffrey pushed the telephone to one side and perched on the edge of her desk.

'I—yes.' She had hardly known where to look. 'Of course—I'm sorry. I—I think——'

'*I* think you should go home. Now,' he said firmly.

'Take your holidays now, Helen. Take two weeks starting today.'

'But——' Her protest was cut off, and had she been looking at her boss's eyes she would have seen the concern in them.

'Take three weeks, four if you feel you need that long. You can't go on like this.'

She looked at him then, forcing herself to say something positive. 'I—Geoff, I think I should give you my notice. I'll leave when you find a replacement.'

'Nonsense! I don't want a replacement. There's nothing wrong with you that a damn good rest won't cure.'

'But I'm inefficient and——'

'Temporarily, yes. But it is only temporary. Look at me, Helen. Look at me and listen.'

She looked at him. He was tall and distinguished with greying hair and superb dress sense, a warm and friendly man whom she respected and liked. She listened, too, feeling grateful for all he was saying and yet strangely detached, as if his words concerned someone else and not herself.

'Two years ago I hired you not only because you were pleasing to the eye, with a ready smile and just the sort of personality that would fit in here, but also because you are an intelligent and sensitive girl with a real feeling for art. You coped beautifully with exhibitors and customers alike. You learned a great deal in a short time. I could take time off and know that the business was in good hands, that you were capable of running the gallery in my absence.'

His smile was replaced by a look which was bordering on pity, something she had seen a great deal of in the last few weeks. 'And now you can't even put an ad in the paper. You can't type a letter without doing it three times.'

And last week she had arranged the shipment of some paintings, the wrong paintings, to a customer in New Zealand. But Geoffrey wasn't reminding her of that blunder.

'Go away somewhere,' he said. 'Forget everything and everyone for three or four weeks. My wife will come in full time while you're away, and I've got John to help me, so don't worry about that.'

Geoffrey looked at her expectantly, waiting, wanting a reaction. When none was forthcoming, he grew irritated. 'For God's sake, Helen, *stop* bottling things up! If you can't talk to me about it, talk to someone else. Just *do* something. It's been four months since your father died and not once have you mentioned his name to me. And look at you! Right now you're on the verge of tears, but you just won't let go. Give in to it, Helen. Dammit, I wish you'd start screaming about it, about the whole stinking business—and I mean screaming. You're being destroyed by your own sensitivity, by your own courage! You could go up north and talk to your brother. He'll understand. He's suffering, too.'

Helen looked down at the floor. No, she couldn't do that. Her brother, Howard, was coming up to his final examinations at university and he had had more than enough upset without her adding to it. Of course Howard was suffering—and coping with his sister's weakness was the last thing he needed right now.

Was it weakness? This anger, rage, that was bottled up inside her, could it be described as weakness? Surely it was only natural? But when, *when* would it start to lessen? Would there ever be a day when she knew a release from the emotion which was locked like a vice around her heart?

'I can't,' she muttered. 'I can't disturb Howard. It wouldn't be fair. His exams——'

'Then go away somewhere. Go home, now, pack a suitcase and take yourself off somewhere. Anywhere.'

The next thing she knew, Geoff was handing her her coat. Dazed, feeling a curious mixture of gratitude and fear, she allowed him to help her into it. Then he picked up her handbag from the floor near her chair, glancing at the brown paper package on her desk as he did so. 'What's that?'

Helen looked at the large brown envelope, having no idea what was inside it. For seconds she could not for the life of her remember what she had put in there; her mind was refusing to function, not that that was anything new.

'Is it something for the post?' Geoff went on. It was only when he picked it up and read out the name written on the front of it that everything fell into place. 'Corinne Clayman . . . there's no address.'

'Oh, yes, that's right.' Helen took the envelope from him. 'It's a handbag. I found it on the street about an hour ago when I went out for a sandwich. I was going to hand it in to a police station, but there was a card inside, a business card from the bank across the road. It seems that whoever owns the bag—this Mrs Clayman—has an appointment with the manager at ten o'clock on Monday. It was written on the card.'

'Isn't there an address inside? A driving licence perhaps?'

She shook her head. 'Only a few credit cards. There's a lot of money—about three thousand American dollars, two pieces of jewellery which look wildly expensive, a pressed flower and a set of keys.' She shrugged. 'But there's no hint of an address. Anyhow, I'll drop it off at the bank now, assuming she has got an appointment. If so, they'll probably know where she can be contacted.'

Helen had done just that, ascertaining that Mrs Clayman did have an appointment with the bank manager before she left it in their safekeeping. She had sealed the envelope with Sellotape and had given it to one of the bank clerks, whom she knew by sight.

She thought no more about the handbag, she was too busy going over all Geoffrey had said to her as she made her way home. If only she could do as he wanted, if only she could start screaming out her anger and hurt over the rotten deal life had given to her father just a few short months ago. Life? Death. Anthony Good had died as a result of what had happened to him, and nothing on earth, no crying or screaming, would alter that fact.

Her boss's other suggestion was more feasible, more helpful. Maybe it would be a good thing to take herself off somewhere for a couple of weeks. Maybe a holiday would help her to put things, life, back into perspective? It was with this thought that she was occupied as she travelled home.

When she got to Reading, she actually did something positive. She went into a department store and bought a handful of cotton tee-shirts and a couple of skirts, not bothering to try them on. But it was a start. The next question was, where would she go? Anywhere. Anywhere warm and quiet, away from the madding crowd, away from civilisation, if that were possible. She had more than enough money for a decent holiday. She could go anywhere she wanted—if she could just make a decision as to a destination.

But the idea of a holiday, the glimmer of hope that the idea had brought, had blown up in her face when she finally got home late in the afternoon. She had walked into her home, the last in a row of detached houses in a quiet lane, to find that it had been wrecked.

There had been little enough for the burglars to take, but they had made off with a few things which were easy to carry—or rather, easy to sell, as the police had pointed out. The police had asked all sorts of questions and she supposed, later, that she had answered them satisfactorily. Was everything insured? they had asked. What time had she left the house? What time had she got home? Would she give them a list of things which were missing?

Among the missing items, and the things Helen cared most about, were her mother's engagement ring and wedding ring. She was not worried about anything else—except the destruction of things which held sentimental value for her. Her father had been an active member of the local amateur dramatic society and in his study there were more than a dozen photographs of him in different plays. They had been hurled against his desk, smashed to bits.

But memories could not easily be destroyed. As she had walked from room to room, looking at the débris, the records, books and clothes which had been strewn around, she had clung to the memories of happy times with her father when she had helped out at the Dramatic Society. She had kept strictly out of the spotlight, working on the scenery and helping with the props. It had been a good laugh, a lot of fun, and though her father had been very disappointed when she had dropped out of university, they had been close during the past two years, they had had quite a lot in common—including a love of music.

Long after the police had gone, Helen had sat on the floor of the living room amidst the pile of records which had been thrown around. Some of the sleeves had been torn, some of the records forcibly bent, but most of them were intact. It was, for the main part, as if the burglars had given vent to their frustration by mindlessly damaging what they could. It was an ordinary three-bedroomed house, quite average inside, and there had been little worth stealing, even if the exterior of the house had led the thieves to think otherwise.

Even the kitchen had not remained untouched. The refrigerator door had been broken off its hinges, full pints of milk had been poured on to the floor and the contents of the freezer tipped out. It was for the hundredth time that Helen had told herself she would never, ever, understand the mentality of some of the creatures who passed as human beings.

However, of itself this incident should not have seemed like the end of the world. But it did. Had her father been around, she would have coped with it well enough. But he was not around. If she had not felt so wretchedly ill, so *tired*, she might not have sat on the floor for hours, staring into space.

It was only when the doorbell started ringing incessantly, in one long, shrill drone, that she became aware of where she was, what she was doing, and what had happened.

'Someone is at the door.' She said the words aloud in an effort to make herself understand them. Still it was minutes before she actually got to her feet and answered the ring.

She opened the door to find a total stranger, a woman, looking at her with a mixture of apology and puzzlement. 'I'm so sorry to ring like that, but I could see you were in——' Helen looked at the woman blankly, her thoughts disconnected from one another and hardly relevant. She was thinking that every light in the house was on, that it was dark outside, that her curtains were open. She was thinking also that the woman was attractive, if exceptionally tall—almost six feet tall. She was wondering why a door-to-door saleswoman would go around wearing a full-length sable coat, and that last thought prompted her to speak. 'I'm not—I mean, I don't want anything, thank you.'

The woman frowned. 'You are Miss Good, aren't you? Miss Helen Good?'

New information was being thrust upon Helen, but she still couldn't make much sense of it. The woman knew her name; she had an unfamiliar accent, she was wearing expensive perfume and just a little too much of it. 'What? Who are you?' she asked wearily.

'I'm Corinne Clayman,' the woman smiled. 'The person whose pocketbook you found today.'

'What?'

'The—you found my pocketbook in the street at lunch time today, I understand.'

'Pocket——?' The woman was American. 'Oh, you mean your handbag. Yes, yes, I——'

'Are you all right?'

'Yes, I——' The doorframe, the outside light and the woman started weaving slightly and the next thing Helen knew was that she was being led into the living room, a strong hand holding her firmly by the elbow.

'My God! What's happened?' Corinne Clayman

gasped when she saw the state of the room. 'Here . . . have you any brandy in the house?'

Helen didn't answer. She had no idea whether there was any brandy in the house. Corinne found it. Corinne encouraged her to take two large gulps of it and Corinne made coffee. She also talked to Helen, she talked until Helen's mind started functioning and she was able to get herself partially together, at least.

The first half hour in the company of Corinne Clayman was strange. As the evening unfolded, things got stranger as far as Helen was concerned. She couldn't remember exactly what she'd said as she answered the woman's questions, when she had first started to talk. There had been a few moments when she had been left alone, when Corinne said something about having a word with the driver who was waiting for her in a car outside.

And then she was back, taking over completely, asking whether the police had been, whether the fingerprint men had been and—incongruously—whether Helen had had anything to eat.

'No, I—oh, please don't bother doing that, Mrs Clayman. It's kind of you, but——'

'It's no trouble at all. And please call me Corinne.' The sable coat had been flung carelessly over an armchair and she was moving deftly around the living room, picking up ornaments, gathering the records together, straightening upturned dining chairs.

After that, she moved on to the kitchen and Helen could hear the sound of broken glass being swept up, of cupboard doors opening and closing. And all the time Corinne was talking, saying she knew exactly how Helen felt, that she too had had a similar experience in her house in Los Angeles *and* in her apartment in New York. 'It's a nasty feeling,' she called, 'knowing that someone has been through all your belongings. In my case they'd even rifled through my lingerie and on the floor of the living room they'd left a particularly vile . . . calling card. It's jealousy, you know. A psychiatrist once told me that when they do things like that . . .'

She went on, but Helen didn't hear all of it. All she wanted to do was lie down and die, that was how tired she felt.

'You were saying you were going on your holidays, Helen. Is your flight some time tomorrow?'

'Was I?' Helen was still sitting on the settee, nursing the brandy glass which had been refilled for the second time. She couldn't remember what she had said. She wanted to explain, now, that she had nothing planned except an idea. Instead she found herself saying, 'I can't stay here tonight. I just can't!' Dear Lord, it had been bad enough living alone in this house for the past four months, but now . . . now . . . this was the last straw. It really was.

'Do you live alone?'

Helen looked up to find Corinne standing in the doorway. She moved over to the sideboard and picked up a small photograph of Anthony and Howard.

'Yes. That's—that's my father. He—died on Christmas day.'

Corinne turned quickly to look at her, her eyes sympathetic. 'And the young man?'

'My brother.'

'I see. Shouldn't you call him, ask him to come over here?'

'I—he's miles away. He's at university, and besides, I—don't want him to know about this. He'd be very upset.'

'Get your coat,' Corinne said suddenly. 'You're coming with me.'

'What?'

Corinne joined her on the settee, smiling. 'You can spend the night with me. I've got a suite at the Dorchester, and there's a spare room. We'll have dinner in the suite and then you'll have a decent night's sleep. Forgive me, but you look as if you need it.'

'I couldn't——'

'It's the least I can do. Look,' she reached for her handbag, the one Helen had handed in to the bank, 'I came here tonight to give you this.' From her bag she took out a white envelope which she waved briefly before tucking it away again. 'It's money.'

'But I don't want——'

'No—I know. But I wanted to thank you. Now I see I can thank you in another way. Come on.'

There was so much Helen wanted to say, so many questions she wanted to ask—like how Corinne had found her, for one thing. Instead she found herself being helped to her feet and fifteen minutes later she was sitting on the back seat of a black Jaguar, being driven by Corinne's chauffeur into the heart of London. It was only then that she looked properly at the woman by her side. She could have been aged anywhere between thirty and forty, it was hard to judge. Her grooming was immaculate and there was about her an aura of wealth which would have showed even without the sable coat and the chauffeur-driven car. She was also beautiful, blonde and brown-eyed with a creamy skin which was flawless.

Helen never did discover exactly who she was, or what she was, except that she was a visiting American who was spending the next month or so in London. That, and the fact that she was a widow. Yet somehow she managed to find out quite a bit about Helen; she already knew about her working at the gallery—which was how she had got Helen's home address, from Geoff Mortimer. And she had been referred to the gallery by the bank clerk to whom Helen had handed the lost handbag.

It had been during dinner in the hotel suite that this explanation had been forthcoming. Helen had picked at her food, but made little resistance when Corinne insisted she drank some wine. Somewhere in the recesses of her mind it had occurred to her that she was imposing on this stranger's hospitality. Dimly, she also had the thought that she could even be behaving irresponsibly, that she didn't know Corinne Clayman from Adam, that the woman might have some obscure and devious reason for taking Helen in hand like this.

She could not quite make sense of that last thought;

she knew only that if Corinne had been a man, things would not have worked out the way they did. But why be suspicious? Was it merely the way Helen had been brought up, by parents who were a little ... proper ... or was it that Corinne's generosity was disproportionate to the so-called kindness Helen had done for her? And Helen felt that it was disproportionate, especially when Corinne offered her the use of the villa she owned in the West Indies, the Bahamas.

But Corinne Clayman had what could only be described as a strong personality. She was also very likeable and pleasant. Besides, Helen was too tired—she just didn't *care* enough—to put up much resistance. Quite apart from that, the description of the villa and its secluded setting sounded perfect, exactly the sort of escape Helen was very much in need of.

'I very rarely go there myself.' Corinne lit a cigarette as the waiter came in to clear the débris of their dinner. 'And the house is just standing there, empty. I let one or two friends use it, but at the moment it's empty, so you might just as well make use of it, Helen. I don't know why you're hesitating. In fact, you'll be doing me a favour. You can see that everything's okay and you'll be giving the servants something to do—looking after you. There's a couple who run the place for me. They have their own accommodation in the grounds at the back.'

'It's really very kind——' Helen began, yawning from the effect of the brandy and the wine.

'Kind? My dear, you have no idea how grateful I am to you! Never in my life have I been careless enough to lose my belongings. I was absolutely distraught when I discovered I'd lost my pocketbook.' She smiled. 'I mean my handbag. It was when I got back to the hotel. My chauffeur and I had called at umpteen shops and offices and I was loaded with carrier bags, a briefcase and heaven knows what, and I just couldn't believe it! I had no idea where to start looking, then I got a call from the bank. I then asked to speak to the teller you'd given the bag to and—well, you know the rest.

'There are things in that bag which are priceless to me—the jewellery. It was given to me by my late husband, and no money in the world could replace those items.'

Helen nodded. She knew exactly what she meant—she was thinking about her mother's stolen rings.

'And you were not only honest enough to hand the bag over, you were also kind enough to give it to the bank—which meant I got it back straight away. You were also thoughtful enough to seal it in an envelope so nobody else could look through its contents.'

Helen smiled, shrugging. 'Anyone would have——'

'No way! Anyone would *not* have. This could never have happened in New York. I'd have said goodbye to the lot by now! I can't tell you how refreshing I find this, which is why I wanted to come and see you personally, to thank you face to face.'

'I'm glad you did.' Helen sighed, knowing a rush of gratitude at being taken away from her house for the night. 'And now if you'll excuse me, I'm very tired.'

'Sure. Now, Trinini is not the easiest place in the world to get to and—have you got a visa for the States?'

'I have, actually, but I'd really like to think about all this.'

Helen said nothing else. She went to bed thinking that she would sleep on the idea. She did sleep, too, albeit in brief snatches. It was with mild surprise that, when she woke and went into the sitting room at nine a.m., she found Corinne Clayman already up and dressed and talking to someone on the telephone. She beckoned the younger girl into the room and Helen sat at the writing desk, her fingers strumming nervously on its smooth surface.

'Ah!' Corinne said at length. 'And how are you feeling today?'

'Much better, thanks. And I've decided to accept.'

'Accept?'

'About the villa.'

Corinne waved a dismissive arm. 'But of course! I've

already made the travelling arrangements! You'll fly to
Florida and take a private plane over to the island.
There are other routes and means—and it's particularly
lovely to go by sea—but I thought you'd want to take
the quickest way.'

There was an argument, then, about money. Corinne
wanted to pay the air fare, but Helen put her foot down
firmly. That was going too far. Corinne gave in, but
only because Helen said she would not go at all if the
older woman insisted on paying her fare.

The next few hours passed in a kind of daze as far
as Helen was concerned. She and Corinne went back
to the house so Helen could get her passport and
pack a suitcase. She also wrote a hasty note to her
boss, telling him to expect her when he saw
her—within reason. But she told him nothing else. All
explanations could wait till she went back to work.
Nor did she explain herself in the quick letter she
wrote to Howard, other than saying she was going on
a hastily planned holiday.

She came downstairs to find that Corinne had
finished the cleaning up job she had started the night
before. The house looked almost normal, even if it
didn't feel normal. 'I—I just don't know how to thank
you, Corinne.' Impulsively, she kissed her cheek briefly,
and was immediately sorry because the older woman
looked a little embarrassed by the gesture.

'Ships that pass in the night, Helen. We're just two
strangers exchanging one kindness for another.' She
took the letters from Helen's hands, offering to mail
them for her. Helen handed over the cheque she had
written for the air fare, which Corinne accepted, and all
the time she was thinking what a strange encounter this
had been. They would never see each other again. There
had been something about Corinne's remark about
ships that pass in the night which had communicated
this knowledge to Helen.

And so it was that she did not ask for Corinne's
home address in America, and it was not offered to her.
Nor did she ask any questions about Corinne and what

she was doing in London. And nothing was volunteered.

Nevertheless they chatted about all sorts of things on the way to the airport—mainly about the island, though, and some fourteen hours later Helen had landed on Trinini Island, had been collected from the tiny aerodrome by the couple who looked after the villa, and had been astonished at the villa's size, its beauty and casual luxury.

After her arrival she had spent four days getting acclimatised, sleeping in snatches to rid herself of jet-lag, and eating not because she wanted to but because she knew she must.

Now, on her fifth day, Helen felt so much better that she was able to acknowledge that she felt better. She was actually starting to think again. She still felt physically tired, but what of it? She had bags of time in which to regain her stamina.

She poked around in her beach bag for her watch. It was lunch time. Any minute now Lizzy would appear at the top of the stone steps leading to the villa, waving to her to signal that her meal was ready. She went indoors, leaving her beach towel where it was. Today she would have an hour's sun after lunch; so far she had sunbathed only during the mornings, and very cautiously, from necessity. For one with such dark hair, so black it was almost blue-black, Helen's skin was very white and burned easily. But her skin had turned from white to pink to a light tan over the past few days, and now her big blue eyes did not look quite so big. Or was that because her face had filled out a little due to the few pounds she had regained since she'd been here?

Whatever, she looked more like her old self, not thin but slim. Inwardly, however, very little had changed other than the steadying of her mind. She still felt sick at heart, outraged, when she thought of what had happened to her father, and she still could not muster any enthusiasm for life. Oh, she could acknowledge detachedly the beauty of her surroundings here, but she was not moved by it. During the past four months she seemed to have lost the ability to *feel*. Nothing saddened her; nothing made her happy. Her emotions were just locked in a sort of vacuum.

She threw her sun-hat on to a chair and ran her fingers through her hair, which was straight and silky and shoulder-length. Lizzy appeared, asking whether she wanted to eat straight away or take a shower first, and Helen settled for the latter.

Both Lizzy and her husband, Lloyd, were natives of the island and obviously proud of their jobs. It wasn't just that they had little to do, there being so few visitors to the villa, it was also the fact that they had their own small house in the grounds, the near reverence in their voices when they mentioned 'Missuhs Clayman'. The couple were in their forties, friendly, eager to please and yet tactful. They left Helen alone completely, except when they were preparing food for her or cleaning the villa, which was just what she wanted. Twice when they had wanted to go off somewhere for the evening they had checked with her first, to make sure that she did not mind.

If they had thought it either odd or unusual that the villa should be occupied by an unknown English girl, and one who wore socks when she sunbathed, they had given no sign of it. Everything seemed, to them, to be wonderful, and Helen envied them their ability to see life that way, their ability to smile and laugh so readily.

'More sunbathing, missy?' Lizzy's eyebrows rose when Helen announced her intention to go back to the beach when she'd finished lunch. 'You don't normally go in the afternoon.'

Helen got up from the table, smiling in spite of herself. 'I'm trying to catch up with you, Lizzy.' At which Lizzy laughed so heartily that it was almost a cackle.

'Oh, Miss Helen! You got a long way to go!'

'Listen, I only want to stay out there for an hour. If I don't come back in, I'll have fallen asleep. If that happens, will you come and wake me, please, Lizzy? I don't want to get burned to a cinder.'

Having been assured on this, Helen went back to the beach. It was just as well she had asked this of Lizzy, because she fell asleep almost instantly. As she drifted off, she was thinking about the villa. It had five bedrooms, two of which were on the upper floor and three were on the ground floor, opening on to the wide terrace which skirted the house. All the rooms were beautifully, comfortably furnished, as was the living room/dining area—a vast room which was split level, the dining area being on the lower level and overlooking the back of the house. The design was super because this room ran the depth of the house and in the evenings one could take coffee in the lounge area, which overlooked the bay.

There were no personal little touches in the house which indicated the personality of Corinne, apart from the paintings which were obviously to her own taste. But there was not so much as a comb or a bottle of perfume or any other little thing that a woman might leave in her second home—or her third home. Still, she had said she came here infrequently, had not been here for a long time.

There were, however, two things about the place which struck Helen as odd—or unexpected, at least. Firstly, there was no telephone. She had been informed by Lloyd that he had known of her arrival because Missuhs Clayman had telephoned the yacht club, who took messages for the villa and whose phone could be used at any time, should Helen wish to make a phone call. So, since there were telephone lines to the island, why didn't Corinne have one installed in the house?

Secondly, there was a grand piano—a white, full grand piano, of all things, in the lounge. How on earth had it been brought to the island? Helen had been surprised to find a freezer in the kitchen and numerous other signs of modernisation and civilisation around the place—but a grand piano?

There was also a hi-fi unit, an enormous collection of

records and cassettes ranging from jazz to classical, and some of them were unlabelled, marked only with a date or a note such as 'Studio II' or 'Gig with Joe at the Lighthouse'.

Had Helen's curiosity been strong enough, she might have questioned Lizzy and Lloyd about these things. But it wasn't that strong and, somehow, she felt that she owed it to Corinne to allow her to remain partially anonymous if that was what she wanted. It would be nothing more than nosiness if Helen were to question her benefactor's employees.

She slept lightly.

There were moments when she rose to the surface of wakefulness, anxious as to how long she had lain in the sun. Then she remembered that she could rely on Lizzy to wake her, and she drifted off again.

It was when a shadow fell across her, blotting out the sun, that she woke up properly, if somewhat groggily. For seconds she was blinded by the sunlight, unable to see anything but a tall, indiscernible figure. She squinted up at it, realising it was neither Lizzy nor Lloyd.

It was a man, a white man, a stranger. He towered over her, his eyes moving swiftly down her body and coming to rest at the socks she was wearing, which must have looked ludicrous to him.

Helen felt neither alarm nor embarrassment, nor did she feel irritated when the man snapped at her in a voice of an unusually deep timbre, an attractive, dark brown voice.

'This is a private beach. There's a notice up there that indicates that fact plainly enough.' He waved an arm towards the notice at the start of the beach, near the steps which led up to the villa.

'Yes, I know, I——' Helen was struggling to her feet when he spoke again, even more sharply than before.

'So you can read?'

'Yes, I can read.' She looked up at him. She was standing now, all five feet five of her, but he still dwarfed her by six inches or more.

She could feel the man's annoyance as he stared at her briefly before turning to walk away, leaving her with an impression of angry eyes, very green eyes, in a face that was deeply tanned. Unsure quite what to say, she hesitated, her eyes on the back of his head as he walked away. 'Just a minute!'

He stopped in his tracks, turning, his hand going up to rake the hair back from his forehead. He had a magnificent head of hair, mid-blond, straight and thick—but too long at the back.

As she moved towards him she realised where he must have come from; there was a boat, a yacht, moored to the jetty stretching into the water at the curve of the bay. He had been walking in that direction. He wasn't alone, either; she could see two figures on the yacht, both looking in her direction.

'I'd like a word with you,' she said as she approached him.

'Oh, yes?' He stuck his hands on his hips, his stance aggressive, his voice cynical. 'About what?' He looked away impatiently before bringing his eyes back to hers, then he nodded sharply as if he'd just realised something.

'I came here for some privacy,' he spat out, 'and I can't imagine how you've managed to track me here, but you're wasting your time. Why the hell can't you leave me alone?'

Helen's mouth opened in astonishment, but he spoke before she did, and as he did so his eyes moved insolently over her from head to foot. 'I'll say this once, just once. I'm not interested in talking to you.' His eyes moved to the soft swell of her breasts in the scanty bikini bra. 'That—or anything else. So take off, will you? Take your big blue eyes, your kinky socks and your pretty little body, and get the hell out of here!'

And with that he turned and headed for the yacht, leaving Helen dumbfounded, staring after him.

CHAPTER TWO

HELEN couldn't believe what she had just heard. She couldn't imagine what it was all about. Had he mistaken her for someone else? What on earth . . .?

For almost a minute she stood watching the retreating figure. She shook her head, hurrying to retrieve her belongings from the sand. She had to find Lizzy—quickly. The only sense Helen could make of all this was that this beach was not so private, after all. Maybe a few other people were entitled to use it? There were villas on either side of the one she was occupying, but they were both several hundred yards away and presumably had their own stretches of beach.

It was about this that she had wanted to talk to the man. The yacht he had arrived in—presumably arrived in—was moored at the point between Corinne's villa and the next. Maybe he had made some kind of mistake? It didn't make sense!

She hurried up the steps, keeping to the shade of the palm trees and calling Lizzy's name even before she got indoors. But Lizzy was not around. Helen moved from room to room, looking for her, eventually going down to her house. There was no sign of her.

When she came back to the villa, she almost collided with Lizzy, who was coming out of the kitchen. 'Oh, Lizzy! I've been looking for you!'

The older woman beamed at her. 'Yes, missy. And I was looking for you! Mr Scot's arrived!'

'Mr Scot?'

Lizzy looked over the younger woman's shoulder and Helen turned to see Lloyd coming in, with a suitcase in either hand. He was followed by another man, who looked like an islander, and was carrying two cardboard cartons. Another black man appeared, also carrying things, and he was followed by a little girl of about five.

The similarity between the child and the man Helen had encountered on the beach was obvious. She was a gorgeous little thing with blonde hair, much lighter hair than his, and positive green eyes. She looked bewildered, almost afraid, and her skin had an unhealthy pallor.

Despite her own confusion, her disappointment at this invasion, Helen had the presence of mind to speak to the child. 'Hello,' she said gently. 'I'm Helen.'

The child said nothing.

'And you must be Samantha!' Lizzy moved eagerly forward and the child stepped back just as the man appeared. Mr Scot, presumably.

'It's all right, honey,' he said to the little girl, 'this is Lizzy. I've been telling you about her, remember?' But as he spoke, it was Helen he was looking at. For a moment he was distracted by Lizzy who, to Helen's surprise, hugged him as if he were a long-lost friend.

'We didn't know you were coming, Mister Scot! How come you didn't let Lizzy know you were coming?'

'I didn't know myself, Lizzy. By rights I should be elsewhere—Disneyland, to be precise.'

'Disneyland?'

There followed a mad minute during which everyone seemed to be talking at once. Lizzy was fussing over the child, telling Mr Scot how pleased she was to meet his daughter, at last; the little girl complained she was thirsty, and Lloyd and the other men went outside.

Helen sank into a chair, looking on and knowing only a sense of disappointment which was increasing by the second. Whoever the man was, he was very welcome here as far as Lizzy was concerned. He was also extremely familiar with the place. As he spoke to Lizzy, he took some keys from his pocket and unlocked the tall, built-in cupboards behind the bar in a corner of the lounge area.

'Take Sam into the kitchen, will you, Lizzy? Give her a drink of juice.' He turned to Helen. 'I think you and I had better talk.' Then, gesturing towards the array of bottles in the cupboards, 'Perhaps you'd like something stronger than orange juice?'

Helen shook her head, waited patiently until he'd poured himself a drink, and pondered over his accent. He was American, all right, but his accent was nowhere near as pronounced as other American accents she'd heard.

He sat facing her, shrugging apologetically, a grim expression on his face. 'Lloyd was on the boat by the time I got back after talking to you. He tells me you're staying here. He also tells me you're English.'

Helen didn't see the relevance of the last remark, but she nodded. 'Yes. I—tried to tell you that I was staying here.'

'So you did. I'm sorry. I thought you were from—I thought you were someone else. Now, if you——'

'Mister Scot?' Lloyd had reappeared, holding what appeared to be a crate. 'There's nothing else to unload, Mister Scot.'

'Put it on the bar,' the American directed. 'Miss— er—which bedroom are you in?'

When Helen looked at him blankly, he repeated the question. 'Are you upstairs or down?'

'Down. I——' She gestured towards the terrace which led to the downstairs rooms, and the man nodded, telling Lloyd to take all the boxes and cases upstairs.

'How long are you staying here?' he asked her suddenly, his voice almost as curt as it had been earlier.

Helen was unmoved by it. She could see the tension in the set of his broad shoulders, could sense that he was as disappointed by her presence as she was by his. 'I think I'd better explain. I was invited here by Corinne Clayman, the lady who owns this house. We——'

'I'm well aware who owns this place,' he interrupted. He almost smiled. Almost. 'Go on. I didn't know Corrie had any English friends.'

Noting the shortened, softened version of Corinne's name, she continued. 'I can't exactly say we're friends. Well, not—you see, we met in unusual circumstances, briefly, and to cut a long story short she offered me the use of her villa for a holiday.'

He didn't seem at all convinced. 'Seems an odd sort of place to come for a vacation. A young woman alone, I mean. There's so little to do on this island. It's very quiet.'

'Which is just what I wanted,' Helen said evenly. 'I needed . . . I needed a rest. Some privacy, like yourself.'

He looked at her quickly. 'Hey, I've apologised for that. I——'

'It doesn't matter. It really doesn't matter,' she said wearily. And she meant it. She didn't care about his outburst, she didn't *care* about anything except that she was no longer alone here. 'If you have any doubts about what I've just told you, you can ring Corinne Clayman. She's staying at the Dorchester Hotel in London.'

The green eyes studied her carefully. 'I'm well aware of that, too.' He paused, leaving a silence which made Helen slightly uncomfortable as he continued to scrutinise her face.

'I—Corinne didn't say anything about——'

'About my coming here? She didn't know. But this place is at my disposal constantly. I come when I can, which isn't often enough.'

'I take it you and she are good friends?' It sounded like a loaded question, she realised as she spoke.

He realised it, too. He paused before answering. 'You could put it like that, I suppose. And no, I don't doubt what you told me about Corrie. It sounds typical of her. She's a very hospitable lady.'

'Very generous.'

Again he thought before he answered. 'Yes, that, too. Did she—what do you know about Corinne?'

'Very little.' The question struck her as peculiar. 'Just that she's on holiday in England. At least, that's what I gathered. Some kind of shopping spree, was my impression.'

There was the shadow of a smile again, a smile which never reached fruition.

'Mr Scot, may I ask how long you intend to stay here?'

He didn't answer her, he was too busy summing her up. He certainly believes in eye-contact, she thought, meeting his gaze steadily. It was several seconds before she realised that she was doing to him exactly what he was doing to her—assessing, gathering impressions.

And there were so many of them to gather. Helen's interest was well and truly caught. There was tension in his face, but it in no way detracted from his attractiveness; the lines of his features were strong, clear-cut, and in his eyes' there was, now, a softness which surprised her.

'Scot,' he said. 'It's just Scot.'

'Oh. Sorry—I'd assumed that was your surname. Scot . . .?'

'We'll leave it at that, shall we?' he said cryptically. 'And your name?'

'Good. Helen Good.'

'*Good*? Miss—Good?'

She smiled a humourless smile. 'I'm afraid so.'

If she had expected a smile in return, it was not forthcoming. This was a man who had a great deal on his mind, that much was obvious. He had been thinking about other things all the time they'd been talking. He still was. Helen knew it because it was exactly the same with her.

Suddenly he got to his feet, shoving his hands into the pockets of his jeans as he looked down at her. 'I don't know how long I'm staying, Helen. A week, two, three . . . as long as it takes.'

'What?'

'My daughter. What I mean is, I'll stay until I see my daughter fit again.'

'She's been ill?'

'Injured,' he amended. 'She—was in a road accident. She's not been out of hospital long.'

'Oh! I'm sorry. How awful for her—for you.'

A look of pure pain flitted across his eyes, and his hand came up to rub the back of his neck.

Helen stood up. 'I think it's time we came to the point, don't you? I'll leave, all right? Just as soon as I can make arrangements.'

He was obviously relieved, his protest no more than a token attempt at courtesy. 'But why should you? How long have you been here?'

'Five days.'

'Is that all?' He looked around distractedly. 'No, we'll go. In the morning, if it's all the same to you.'

'But——'

'Daddy?' They both turned at the sound of Samantha's voice. She was standing in the doorway to the kitchen, an anxious-looking Lizzy hovering over her. 'Daddy, my head hurts! It's muzzy, and I'm tired!'

Scot was already on his way to her, scooping her high into his arms. To Lizzy he said, 'We'll have dinner at eight o'clock sharp. I'm putting Sam to bed for a few hours in the meantime.' As he reached the foot of the stairs, he said to Helen, 'We'll sort that business out later, okay? Over dinner.'

Helen nodded, shrugging helplessly at Lizzy as Scot took his daughter upstairs.

'Mister Scot will probably have a few hours' sleep, too,' Lizzy put in helpfully.

'Mr Scot comes here regularly, does he?'

'Regular but not often.' Lizzy started straightening the cushions on the settee.

'I wonder why his wife hasn't come with him,' Helen went on, 'that child looks as if she needs to be taken care of.'

She was unsure whether Lizzy was just pretending not to have heard. No answer was forthcoming. More clearly Helen said, 'Lizzy, is he—does he normally come here with Mrs Clayman?'

'Oh, no, missy.' Lizzy looked surprised now. 'He's usually alone. He only came here once with Mrs Clayman—on his first visit a few years ago.'

Helen's interest was very shortlived. And it was clear that Lizzy was reluctant to talk. She retreated to her

room and took a long, cool bath and she tried,
unsuccessfully, to get lost in the book she'd been
carrying around with her for days.

Dinner was a rather stilted affair, as awkward as the
afternoon had been. Scot . . . whatever his name was . . .
had withdrawn into his thoughts, and this in itself
spoke volumes to Helen. She caught herself looking at
him several times, curious, then looking away again in
case he became aware of her curiosity,

He looked quite different from the man she had met
on the beach, whose clothes had been stained with
perspiration, crumpled and a little dusty. The tension
had gone from his face, his hair had been washed and
looked lighter because of it and he was wearing crisp
white slacks and a black cotton shirt, unbuttoned at the
throat. She wondered about his age—thirty-two, thirty-
five, possibly a little more?

There was conversation of sorts. Samantha, who was
obviously feeling better after her sleep, spoke up from
time to time. She was a serious little girl, and the first
thing she told Helen was that she didn't normally stay
up as late as this. .

Helen smiled, grateful that the silence was broken.
'Well, I suppose you're allowed to stay up because you
had a long sleep this afternoon. How old are you?'

'Five and a half and a bit. I'll be six soon. I'm having
my birthday here, Daddy says.' She looked thoughtfully
at Helen. 'How old are you?'

'Samantha . . .'

The warning note in Scot's voice brought Helen's
head up. 'It's all right, I don't mind.' She turned to
Samantha. 'I'm twenty-two . . . and a bit.'

The child's giggle was delightful because it was so
unexpected. Scot, however, was not prepared to leave it
at that. 'It's impolite to ask a lady her age, Sam.'

'She asked me!' There was defiance now.

Helen stepped in quickly. 'Daddy means grown-ups.
It—it doesn't count for little girls.'

Samantha looked uncertainly from one to the other,

but whatever she saw in her father's face subdued her for a while.

'More wine, Helen?'

'Thank you. You—brought this with you, didn't you? It's very good.'

'I think so.' He paused. 'Didn't Corrie tell you where to find a spare key to the cupboard?' He gestured towards the bar. 'You've been here five days without touching a drop of alcohol?'

'Actually, she did say something about a key. I couldn't remember what. But——' Helen looked down at her glass, 'I can take it or leave it.'

He said nothing else. Silence reigned.

'I brought Jemima with me,' Samantha said at length. 'You can see her if you like. But I don't show her to everyone.'

Helen looked at Scot before answering, uncertain whether he would intervene. 'Well, that's very kind. Er—who is Jemima?'

'My doll. We didn't bring Oscar, though. Scot didn't want to bring him.'

Helen's eyebrows went up. Suddenly it was 'Scot', not 'Daddy'. 'And who's Oscar? Your teddy bear?'

'Nooo!' The child flashed a disbelieving look. 'He's Scot's——'

'Eat your food, Sam!' There was no defiance this time. Scot's voice came out sharply, far more than was necessary, in Helen's opinion.

She drank up what was left of her wine. Both she and Scot had finished eating; Samantha was still pushing her food around. 'Scot, Samantha, if you'll excuse me, I'd like to go out on the terrace and get a little air.'

Scot rose from his seat, giving her a deferential bow of the head. The gesture amazed Helen, though she didn't let it show. So! After his vulgar outburst on the beach she was now being referred to as a lady and treated as such! Quite right, too, she thought as she went outside.

He joined her some ten minutes later, a cigarette in

one hand and a brandy glass in the other. 'Can I get you a brandy, Helen?'

'I——yes, thank you.'

Lizzy appeared with a tray of coffee which she put on the white wrought-iron table next to the chair Helen was occupying. Ah, but it was so pleasant out here, the warm night air almost a caress against the bare skin of her arms.

Lizzy stepped to one side as Scot reappeared. 'Thank you, Lizzy,' he said. 'Dinner was just perfect, as usual. Go home when you've finished clearing up.'

'Where's Samantha?' Helen asked him.

'Brushing her teeth. She'll play for half an hour or so before going to bed.' He was standing with his back to her, leaning against the waist-high railing skirting the terrace.

'Sugar, Scot? Milk?'

'Neither.'

He's used to being waited on, she observed, the way he directs the staff, his attitude. Detached but polite.

'Your coffee.'

He sat on the other side of the table, looking across the ocean as he drank.

'There's a light on your yacht,' Helen said at length. 'Is that usual?'

'The crew are on board. The two guys who helped me with the luggage today. They sleep on board.'

'Oh.'

He looked at her directly in that way he had of trying to read her mind. At least, that was what it felt like. 'What would you say if I told you I'm in no mood for small talk?'

'That I'm well aware of it,' she shrugged. 'That makes two of us.'

His sudden smile, the first she'd seen, changed his entire countenance, so much so that she felt an involuntary ripple of surprise—a very pleasant sensation. In the glow of the lights from the lounge, his skin looked even more tanned, his teeth white and strong and even, and his eyes were lit with amusement. 'You're a cool customer, Helen. I wonder what it would take to ruffle you? I'd forgotten how aloof the English can be at times.'

She sighed without realising she was doing so. 'I thought we'd just agreed to cut out the small talk?' She had been waiting for him to bring up the subject of who was going to leave the villa, but he had been miles away in his thoughts over dinner. It was time for her to take the initiative. 'Look, Mr—er—Scot. In the circumstances, I feel I should be the one to leave here tomorrow.'

'As you wish,' he shrugged.

It wasn't as she wished. She was merely doing what she felt she ought to do—since he was obviously a close friend of Corinne's, and Helen was virtually a stranger. But the prospect, the very thought of the journey ahead of her, filled her with dread. She was by no means ready to face it; she had not had enough of this place, not by a long way.

Maybe she would stay in Florida for a couple of weeks? Trinini Island was only a hundred and fifty miles away, give or take a few. Why not? After all, she hadn't spent any money yet, other than her plane fare.

Her silence prompted him to speak. 'You're sure it's what you want?'

'It's for the best,' she said crisply. 'I came here to be alone, to think. Just like yourself.'

'I'm not alone,' he pointed out. With a certain bitterness he added, 'I didn't come here to think—I'm through with that. I've done nothing but think, plan, since Samantha had her accident. I came here to get to know my daughter.'

As if on cue, the child appeared before Helen could say anything. To get to know his daughter? What was that supposed to mean? Who *was* this man? What was he? Why had he refused to mention his surname? She was thinking of his remarks on the beach. He had thought she was someone who had 'tracked' him to the island, someone who wanted something from him. And, judging by his scathing and vulgar remarks, he had seemed to think she was prepared to pay a price for what she wanted!

A big rag doll was plonked on Helen's knee. 'Jemima!'

'Indeed? Gosh, she's lovely, isn't she?' Helen touched the nose which was a button on the doll's face. Its long hair, its fringe, were a series of tightly plaited cottons, straight and black.

'She's like you!' Samantha observed. 'Helen, she's just like you! Look at her hair!'

'Samantha . . .'

'Thank you.' Helen feigned pleasure at the little girl's compliment, because it had been meant as a compliment, speaking quickly before her father could admonish. She had observed over dinner how frequently he stopped the child from chattering, but she had thought it was because he considered it out of order at table.

Unlike her father's, Samantha's hair was curly, much finer. Helen put out her hand, twirling one of the curls, noting the child's look of pleasure as she did so. 'I bet Jemima would rather have hair like yours, its much prettier.'

'Why do you talk funny?' asked the little girl.

'Because I come from——'

Scot got to his feet, his voice holding just a tinge of impatience. 'I think it's bedtime, Sam.'

'Because I come from another country,' Helen went on determinedly. If Scot was trying to protect her from the child's curiosity, he needn't bother. She didn't mind it in the least. 'I come from a place called England.'

'England!' Samantha patted her hand against her father's thigh. 'We're going to England, aren't we, Daddy? We're going after we've been to Disneyland!'

'If you'll excuse me,' he said to Helen, picking his daughter up.

Helen handed her the doll. 'Goodnight, Samantha. It was lovely meeting you.'

She heard the bombardment of questions her parting shot had provoked as he took the little girl indoors and up the stairs. She did not, however, hear the answers.

She drained her brandy glass, finding herself annoyed by the scene. She had realised, now, that Scot was not protecting her from Samantha's curiosity, he'd whisked the child away because she had been saying things he didn't want Helen to hear!

What the devil was the matter with the man? Was his forthcoming visit to England a State secret or something? If he were here to get to know his daughter, as he'd said, then he'd do well to try encouraging her to talk instead of shutting her up every time she opened her mouth!

Irritated, Helen got up and headed for her room. There was no point in hanging about on the terrace when he would no doubt return. As far as she was concerned, their business had been settled; she would leave Trinini Island some time tomorrow.

She closed the slats on her blinds as soon as she got into her room. The windows opened on to the terrace and she left them open, assured of privacy once the slats were closed. She went into the adjoining bathroom which was situated between her room and the next bedroom, still distracted from the things which were usually on her mind.

As she got into bed, a long way from sleepiness, she heard Scot going out to the terrace. A few minutes later he went indoors.

This time, Helen got into her book. She read until she was drowsy, the hands on her travelling alarm clock telling her it was turned midnight.

She woke some time later, thrust into consciousness by the sound of a voice crying out. It was her own voice. She was soaked in perspiration, her hands trembling as everything came into focus and she remembered the dream, the nightmare. The recurring nightmare. Dear. God, when would it stop haunting her?

Now, the luminous hands on her clock told her it was almost four a.m. She shivered, reaching for her robe as she got out of bed. What she needed was a drink, something sharp and cold. There was lemonade in the fridge.

She unlocked her bedroom door and padded, barefoot, along the terrace to the big sliding glass doors which opened into the lounge. These doors were never locked, but she was surprised to find them open, until she saw the glow of a table lamp and realised that Scot was in the lounge.

He looked at her, his eyes narrowing thoughtfully.

'So you couldn't sleep, either,' she stated in an effort to fend off any remarks he might be about to make. 'It must be the heat.'

'It's not that hot,' he pointed out. 'And my mistake was in taking a long siesta this afternoon. But you were sleeping, Helen. You were thrashing about in there, almost screaming at one point. I was in two minds whether to come in and wake you.'

He couldn't have come into her room; the door was locked. She consoled herself with that knowledge but made no comment about it. 'That would not have been appreciated,' she said quickly, heading for the kitchen.

The coolness of the tiled floors was welcome. She closed the kitchen door behind her, wiping her clammy hands against her robe. The lemonade bottle was half full and icy against the heat of her palms. She filled a glass, drank it straight off and refilled it. But the glass slid from her grasp and shattered noisily on the floor. With a groan, she stooped to pick up the pieces, unable to stop the trembling of her hands.

'Allow me.' Scot was walking towards her, and she straightened, perfectly happy to let him mop up the mess.

She leaned against the refrigerator, her acknowledgement perfunctory. 'Thank you.'

When he had finished he took hold of her by the arm, and the shock of the contact brought her eyes wide open.

'Take it easy,' he ordered. 'Go and sit down. I want to talk to you. I'll bring you another drink.'

For some obscure reason it never occurred to her to argue about it. She did as he bade her, one hand going unconsciously to touch the place where he had held her.

This time he sat next to her on the huge white sofa which of itself must have cost a small fortune. She took the glass he offered and edged away from him, suddenly conscious that she was wearing a robe and nothing else. Which was silly really; he'd already seen her nearly naked in her bikini. Nevertheless she held one hand against the neckline of her robe as she drank.

'Perhaps this will make you feel better.' Scot spoke quietly, almost gently, as he moved away from her to sit in an armchair.

It did, and she told him as much.

'You look like death,' he said at length.

'Thanks!'

His smile was fleeting. 'I don't know what's on your mind, but it's something heavy, that's for sure.'

When she made no reply, he went on, 'Look, this is a big house. Outside, there's a big ocean and a generous amount of beach. Why don't we all stay on? What's the big deal? It's obvious you're in no mood to go back to—whatever it is that's bugging you.'

It was very tempting. Oh, she couldn't escape her troubles, no matter where she was. But it helped, being here. It helped enormously.

Scot stretched his long legs out in front of him, his fingers forming a temple in front of his face as he looked at her, watched her. 'You really have no idea who I am, have you?'

She blinked in surprise. 'Should I have?'

'Women! Why do they always answer a question with a question?'

'Why shouldn't we?'

She hadn't realised what she'd said until he smiled that incredibly attractive smile. But it left her cold this time. 'No, I have no idea who you are, and I'm not interested.'

'Fine, that's just fine.' He leaned forward, propping his chin against his hands. 'I think we've reached an understanding, Helen. We don't like small talk, we have no intention of invading each other's privacy. So why not settle this now: let's both stay on here.'

'It's okay with me,' she shrugged. And it was, too, provided they kept to their understanding. She said as much to him. 'So long as that's firmly understood, then yes, I'm agreeable.' She got to her feet, taking her half empty glass with her.

The deep voice floated over to her as she reached the doors. 'Mind you, I think a reluctance to bid me goodnight is going too far,' he said drily. 'Or should I say good morning?'

'Whatever you like,' she said tiredly. 'And while we're having honest hour and straight talk, let me tell you this: apart from the time of day, you can expect nothing else from me. You see, Mr ... I've come to the conclusion that I don't like you very much.'

He turned around in his chair so he could look at her. 'I can understand that,' he said, without even a trace of amusement. 'Because I don't like me, either. Not one little bit.'

CHAPTER THREE

THEIR arrangement worked out very well. During the first few days, which were during early May, Scot and his daughter went out on the yacht—exploring the surrounding islands, presumably, although Helen did not give the matter much thought.

She lazed around, went for walks and did a small amount of exploring of her own. One morning, realising that Scot and Sam were going to stay on the beach that day, she went with Lizzy and Lloyd to the market where they shopped for food.

There were a couple of hotels on the island, one of which had a nightclub, and of course there was the Yacht Club—all of which she saw from the car. In town she saw only a handful of tourists and she was told by Lloyd that the eastern side of Trinini, small though the island was, was quite densely populated. The sun shone continuously; being May it was hot but by no means unbearably so. Helen's suntan deepened daily, much to Lizzy's delight, but she maintained her caution about over-exposure, knowing that the sun must be treated with respect in this part of the world.

The only contact she had had alone with Scot was during their evening meals. She had toyed with the idea of taking dinner in her room, but had decided that that would be overdoing things. Since Samantha ate earlier and was in bed by the time the adults had dinner, the meals she had shared with Scot so far had been almost silent. Her reaction to him had levelled off from dislike to neutrality; there was, actually, nothing to dislike about him.

Or had her opinion been affected by the effort he was making with his daughter? The child seemed a little happier now, more ready to laugh than she had been at first. She was also looking healthier, her flawless young skin becoming rapidly tanned. Her father tanned easily, too. But then not only did he have that sort of skin, he also had a good foundation; he had been tanned when he arrived on Trinini. He had sailed to the island from Miami, which was where he left his yacht when he wasn't using it. That was one titbit of information he hadn't minded giving her. It occurred to her, as she went round the market with Lizzy and Lloyd, that she had only to ask one question of them and they would tell her what and who Scot was. Or would they?

But it didn't really matter whether they would or not, because on principle Helen wouldn't ask the question. Any more than she would ask about Corinne Clayman. What right had she to pry, to disregard people's wish for privacy? She was, after all, to some extent an interloper, although to be fair, Scot had done nothing at all to make her feel that way.

Chatting to Samantha was something Helen had found not only easy but pleasurable. She was a bright little girl and a little old for her years. She had given Helen an introduction to the other dolls she had brought with her, and a look at her toys and games (the contents of the cartons brought from the yacht). Samantha's room was chaotic, despite the efforts Lizzy made, no doubt, to keep it in some kind of order.

Samantha came out to meet Helen as she was getting out of the car on her return from the market. 'Helen, I thought you'd be on the beach today. We could have played a game! Yesterday I asked Scot if he would take you on the boat with us—and he said no!'

Helen took hold of her hand as she walked towards the back entrance to the villa, looking up to find Scot standing in the doorway.

'I must apologise for my daughter,' he said, his clear green eyes meeting Helen's.

'Don't,' she said. 'Not ever.' Conscious of Samantha's curious look, she let go of her hand. 'Darling, why don't you go and help Lizzy to take the shopping in? She's got something nice for you!'

'Chocolate?'

'Wait and see.'

The child hurried off and Helen's eyes moved back to Scot. For the first time she saw an awkwardness about him, an attitude of uncertainty. 'You're right, I shouldn't do that. Not ever. It's just——'

'It's just that you think she's bothering me.' Helen walked ahead of him into the house. 'Well, she isn't, I assure you. I find her absolutely delightful, for what it's worth.'

'It's worth a lot,' he said evenly. 'It puts my mind at rest, if you're sure——'

'I'm sure.'

She was treated to a smile. She thought of it in those terms because when he smiled it made such a difference to him. It was like the sun suddenly appearing amongst the clouds.

'Can I get you a drink, Helen?'

'Please. I'm gasping for a drink. Is there any beer in the fridge?'

'Coming up!'

She waited in the lounge until he'd brought the glass, her fingers trailing along the smooth wood of the grand piano. 'Thanks.' She nodded towards the instrument. 'I wonder how on earth Corinne got this to the island?'

'With difficulty.'

So there was a sense of humour in him. She sat at the stool, lifting the lid and tinkling at the keys.

'Do you play?' he asked.

She nodded. 'I went through the grades when I was a youngster.' Unaware of the impish look on her face, she added, 'But I'm not saying how many!' Actually, she played moderately well. She had entertained herself with the piano for several hours before he'd come to the island. 'Do you play, Scot?'

'I . . .' he paused, considering her, considering his words before he answered '. . . went through the grades when I was a youngster. But I'm not saying how many.'

If his reply was supposed to amuse her, it failed. Couldn't he answer a straightforward question? What was it with him? Or did he regard this as small talk?

She got up. 'I'll finish my drink in my room.'

'Helen . . .'

'See you at dinner,' she said over her shoulder, keeping her voice light because she did not wish to create an atmosphere.

In her room she regretted what she had done—flouncing off like that. Maybe he had meant it simply as a joke, parroting the exact words she'd used?

Why concern myself? she asked her reflection when she was changing for dinner. Two hours had passed and she was still thinking about the wretched man. Now why was that? Why was he occupying her thoughts so much?

The answer, of course, was as plain as the nose on her face, a face which now had a light scattering of freckles on it, she noted irritably. She never had liked it when her freckles came out in response to sunshine, although people seemed to think they were attractive. Scot was occupying her thoughts because she wanted it that way. Wasn't he something of a mystery and a welcome distraction for her mind? There was no harm in that. On the contrary, she conceded, she was almost grateful to the man!

She eyed her reflection critically, putting on a little more make-up than usual, and the usual was lip-gloss and nothing else. A touch of mascara and eye-shadow was in order tonight, she felt, because the dress she had put on made her look younger somehow, younger and unsophisticated. And she did not want to feel unsophisticated when she was in Scot's company. His own worldliness was stamped all over him and she did not want to feel at a disadvantage.

There was a drink waiting for her on the coffee table when she went into the lounge, something in a tall, frosted glass with bits of fruit crowning the top of it. Two glasses stood side by side and she eyed them, mildly amused. 'Those look good. Er—what are they?'

'Suspicious, aren't you?'

'Isn't that rather like the pot calling the kettle black?' He gave her an exaggerated frown. 'What? An expatriate I might be, but I'm not familiar with that expression!'

Helen was taken aback, to say the least. Had he just volunteered something about himself? And—an expatriate? 'You're *English?*'

'Born and bred. Well, for the first eleven years of my life, at any rate.'

'Well, I never!'

He grinned, enjoying her turn of phrase. 'So what was all that about pots and kettles?'

'I've forgotten,' she lied. 'Can't remember what I was going to say.' She had been about to tell him that *he* was a suspicious devil, suspicious of her for some reason, but since the conversation had turned lighthearted, she let it go.

She looked at him over the rim of her glass as she sipped the drink. He was sprawled in an armchair, one leg hooked casually over the side. In an offwhite suit and a pale blue open-necked shirt he looked more attractive than ever. And the sun had lightened his hair a little. His hair did not behave very well, it was thick and rather wild, maybe because he was in need of a haircut. It was touching his collar at the back, curling slightly where it did so.

'You're looking very pretty tonight, Helen.' His tone was neutral enough, but the words, and the way his eyes swept over her from head to toe, bothered her disproportionately.

To her horror she could feel colour rising in her cheeks. It got worse when she realised he was stifling a smile. Oh, God, how utterly ridiculous! And there she had been, taking pains not to appear unsophisticated!

'How's the cocktail?' he asked.

'I—it's fine. Really good.'

'Glad I've done something right at last.'

'What—do you mean?'

He shrugged his broad shoulders carelessly. 'Just now I embarrassed you, this afternoon I annoyed you, last night I virtually ignored you over dinner and—well, the day I bawled you out on the beach I also insulted you.'

'I told you, it doesn't matter.'

'Then what does matter? What in this world does matter? If we can't behave civilly to our fellow men, don't you think that's a sad state of affairs?'

'Very much so,' she agreed. 'And you surprise me, Scot. I have you labelled as a cynic.'

He did not hesitate. 'You've got it right. You see, I'm a very good judge of character, and with the people who move in my orbit I do well to be cynical. It's a means of protection. But you are not of my world, Helen. You're different—very, very different. Now don't go all shy and blushing on me if I tell you that you're a breath of fresh air.'

She was in earnest when she answered that one. 'I haven't the faintest idea what you're talking about.'

'Suffice it to say that my apology for my attack is sincere.' He held up a hand. 'All right, all right, I shan't mention it again! I just wanted you to know. Now, before we revert to silence, there's something I want to explain. I've recently experienced ... let's call it something of a personality change. But I haven't quite got rid of the old me yet, so—bear with me, will you?'

'The old you? I—is this what you meant when you said you didn't like yourself?'

'Yes,' he said quietly. 'But I'm working on it.' Then, cryptically, 'That and being a better father to my daughter.' And with that he got up and extended his arm to her. 'Since it's getting warmer by the day I thought it would be nice to eat outside from now on. I hope that's okay with you?'

'Of course.' She got to her feet and slipped her hand under his arm. She did that not only because it would have been churlish not to but also because she wanted to. She wanted to meet him halfway. She had understood what he'd said only vaguely, but he had been making an effort to communicate with her and she didn't mind it at all. In fact she appreciated it, she realised with some surprise.

They didn't revert to silence over dinner, though things did not go as smoothly as they might have. There was a power cut just a few minutes after they sat down to eat. The terrace and gardens were lit by a series of lamps during the evenings and when the villa and everything else fell into darkness there was only the light of the moon remaining.

When Helen let out an exclamation of surprise, Scot reassured her at once. 'It happens often. Not to worry, we've got plenty of candles and storm lamps in the house. Excuse me a moment.'

He and Lizzy came on to the terrace a couple of minutes later, placing the oil lamps at strategic points so that the dining table was amply lit. Lizzy went inside again and came back with two lighted candles which she stood on the table, and far from its being an inconvenience the entire setting had suddenly taken on romantic overtones.

No sooner had Lizzy retreated than the lights came on again. Scot looked heavenward and Helen started laughing as he got up to turn off the lamps. 'It's a good job this is a cold meal!' she said, snuffing the candles as Scot sat down again.

'Oh,' he said, 'you might have left the candles. I thought that was a very nice touch—quite romantic.'

And wasted on us, Helen thought. But she made no comment because Scot had not been serious, it was just a throwaway line. Or so she thought.

'No comment?' he asked.

'No comment,' she said coolly.

He grinned at her, the clean green eyes lingering on her face for just a moment longer than was necessary.

He topped up her wine glass. 'About your meeting with Corinne. You said you met briefly, in unusual circumstances. May I ask what they were?'

'Of course.' Helen launched into the story of the handbag and how she had been finishing work that day to start her holidays. That was a slight variation on the truth, but she didn't want to go into too much detail about the state she was in before she came to the Bahamas. She told Scot about the burglary and the way Corinne had rallied, taking over and clearing up for her.

But the fact that she had spent the night with Corinne at the Dorchester provoked questions from Scot which obliged her to explain a little more than she wanted to. 'Well, I—I just didn't want to stay alone in the house that night.'

'You live alone?' When Helen nodded, he went on, 'Have you no family, no friends?'

'Of course I have friends. But they live in London mainly. There's nobody I'm close to in the neighbourhood where I live. And my brother's at university in Lancashire—that's two hundred miles away,' she explained.

'So Corrie took you under her wing.'

'Yes, that's a good way of putting it. She was very kind to me.'

He nodded. 'She's—a fine woman.' Then, 'There's more to this story, isn't there? If you were finishing work to go on vacation, how come you had nothing planned, nothing booked?'

'I . . . was just leaving things till the last minute.'

'In other words, I should mind my own business.'

Helen smiled thinly. 'I didn't say that. It's just—just that I'd been upset about something before the burglary and I wasn't really thinking properly at the time.'

'A love affair gone wrong? It has to involve a man.'

'Has it?' Her smile widened, but it was a sad smile and Scot apologised for prying.

'I'm breaking our agreement, forgive me. For a moment there I—forgot about our pact.'

'I don't mind,' she said honestly. 'In a way, you were right. But the man concerned was my father. He—he died recently, and I hadn't got over it.'

Haven't got over it, she should have said. Would she ever?

'Do you want to talk about it?' he asked quietly.

Helen stiffened visibly. 'I can't.'

Scot was watching her carefully, his eyes gentle and lit by what appeared to be genuine concern. 'It sometimes helps.'

'I know, but—I just can't. Please, Scot, that's enough!'

He did not apologise this time. He changed the subject quickly, but he did so by resorting to small talk, of which they were both well aware.

But Helen didn't mind in the least. She thought, in fact, that it was sweet of him. Although she could not begin to explain it, she had the feeling that a friendship had just been born.

One would not have thought so, however, in the couple of days that followed. Helen got up the following morning to be informed by Lizzy that Scot had gone out on the yacht with Samantha and would be away for the night, maybe two nights.

She felt vaguely disappointed and she chided herself for it. Idiot! She had the place to herself now, hadn't she? Which was precisely what she wanted.

And yet, for the first time since her arrival, she felt dissatisfied with her own company. But the feeling passed after a few hours. She slept during the afternoon and read in the evening, late into the night.

The following day she swam a lot and did a little more exploring inland, by foot. The car was at her disposal, but it was too hot to spend time in the stuffy atmosphere of a car during the day. So she walked. She wore the hat she had bought at the local straw market she had visited with Lloyd and Lizzy, cotton slacks and a loose-fitting shirt, and was more than entertained by the scenery around her.

The sky was a perfect azure, the golden sun beating down in the heat of the afternoon and from time to time she stopped to rest for a few minutes under the shade of the palm trees dotted along the roadside. It was then that her thoughts turned to Scot.

Maybe she should have talked to him. It would be safe talking to someone who was, like Corinne, a ship that passed in the night. When this holiday was over she would never see Scot again, so what did it matter if she did tell him her troubles?

Because she couldn't tell her tale without breaking down, that's what. And the last thing she wanted to do in his presence was to break down and cry.

She headed back for the villa when the sun started sinking in the sky, looking forward to a shower and a long cool drink. Because she went in at the back entrance, she didn't see that the yacht had returned, nor did she expect the feeling of gladness she experienced when she found Scot and Samantha in the lounge. So they had stayed away only the one night, after all.

'Hi!' He waved as she went in through the door. 'Are you wearing that hat for a bet?'

'What a nerve!' she exclaimed, with mock indignation. 'This was handmade by one of the local ladies, if you don't mind. It's unique.' She lifted the big straw hat from her head and put it carefully on the coffee table.

'You can say that again!'

Samantha's greeting was very different. She hurried over to Helen and took hold of both hands, urging her to sit down on the floor, where she was playing a game with her father. They had played several, by the looks of things. There were dice and tumblers and boards all over the floor.

'Scot isn't very good at games,' Samantha complained. 'He's not even good at Snakes and Ladders! Will you play with me, Helen?'

Scot tweaked his daughter's nose, looking indignant. 'Daddy, madam—the name is Daddy. And I just beat you at Snakes and Ladders, didn't I?'

'Yes, Daddy. But only once!'

He looked at Helen. 'Ah, well, that's the luck of the dice. Drink, Helen?'

'Mm, please. A cold beer.' She sat down on the cool tiles of the floor, ruffling Samantha's hair.

'Are you going to play with me?' asked the little girl.

'Yes. As soon as I've had a drink.'

'Don't hassle Helen,' Scot called from the kitchen.

Samantha looked at her uncertainly. 'Is it all right?'

'Yes, darling. I love Snakes and Ladders!' She heard the low, rumbling laughter coming from the kitchen, but she kept her face straight for Samantha's sake. 'Did you have a nice trip on the boat, Sam?'

The answer was a pretty little face being pulled. 'It would have been better if you came with us. Don't you like fishing and looking at the islands and swimming?'

'Well——'

'And picnics,' added Samantha, making it all the more tempting. 'Oh, why don't you come with us? Why do you always want to be by yourself?'

Helen felt well and truly put on the spot. She looked at Scot a little helplessly as he gave her her drink. He raised his eyebrows, his attitude telling her she must answer for herself.

'I—think your father . . .' She floundered.

'Why don't you say you might come with us next time but first you'll have to think about it?' Scot suggested.

Helen said just that.

'And when will you know?' Samantha was dead serious, and Helen burst out laughing.

'How about tomorrow morning? I'll give you my decision then.'

Scot didn't sit down again. 'Helen, would you keep an eye on Sam for a while? I want to have a word with Lloyd, he's on the yacht with the boys.'

'Of course.'

'Daddy isn't going to do any work while we're here, you know,' Samantha announced as soon as he'd left. She looked delighted about it. 'He promised. And we're going to Disneyland. Well, we went to Disneyland before we came here, but I got sick and Daddy was unhappy, and then he met this man and he got angry, and so we came here instead.'

It was not the most coherent of sentences, but Helen got the general drift. 'So you're going back to Disneyland?'

Samantha bobbed her head up and down. 'He promised. And if you promise, you have to do it, don't you?'

Helen thought carefully about that one. 'You must try to, you must try hard.'

'Are you coming with us? To Disneyland?'

'No, darling, I'm afraid not. Shall we play now?'

'In a minute. Bessie didn't want to go, either. But she's very old. She's fifty—that's a lot, isn't it?'

'And who's Bessie?'

'She lives in our house. She does the shopping and makes my dinners. And she takes me to school, and I hate school. I like Bessie, though.' Samantha paused for breath, her head cocked to one side as she watched Helen curiously. 'Why do you call him Scot?'

'Doesn't everyone?'

'Only me and Corinne. But the people who come to our house a lot call him Minestrow.'

'What?'

'Minestrow. Lots of people call him that.'

It didn't make sense to Helen, but in no way was she going to pursue the matter. Minestrow? What was that supposed to convey? She finished her beer, wishing Scot would come back and take over. Samantha's ramblings were making her feel tense, for some reason. Happily, it didn't last. Samantha picked up the dice and Helen was, to her relief, no longer privy to a gush of information, the revelation of which Scot would no doubt disapprove of.

Over dinner that evening he cleared up the business about her joining them on the yacht.

'Sam's continually asking me to take you with us,' he explained. 'And I keep telling her you want to be alone. Needless to say, she doesn't understand that.'

'I think that's a little unfair,' Helen protested. 'I think you should include the fact that *you* want to be alone with her.'

Scot pushed his plate away and lit a cigarette. 'Helen, I've been the worst father in the world, but I'm getting better every day. I think. I've spent so much time working . . .' there was a cynical twist to his lips before he went on '. . . among other things, that she and I hardly knew each other. Being here has cured all that, and your presence has helped somehow. But I don't want to put any onus on you. I'd be delighted if you'd come out with us, but you're free to do as you want, naturally.'

'Are you telling me that *you* wouldn't mind?'

'Mind? I've just told you, I'd be delighted.'

'Then I will—thank you,' Helen told him.

'Thank you.'

There was silence, a comfortable silence in which quite a lot was said.

The friendship would be temporary, of course, but it would be nice while it lasted. And in the last few seconds it had been sealed.

'Let's go out for a drink tonight, Helen. There are a couple of hotels——'

'We'd need a babysitter,' she reminded him.

'Lizzy will be more than happy to fulfil that role. I'll go and have a word with her and tell her where we'll be.' Scot paused as he reached the door to the lounge. 'Why don't you go and see if Sam's still awake? You can give her your—er—decision,' he grinned. 'It'll make her night.'

Samantha was awake, and was delighted at the news. Helen couldn't help laughing, it was good for the ego being in demand like this! She said as much to Scot as they were leaving the villa.

'Come on now,' he said sceptically. 'A girl like you? I shouldn't think your ego's in much need of a boost.'

That's where he's wrong, Helen thought. She had been at her lowest ebb for the past four months, neither giving nor receiving pleasure to or from anyone. Or anything.

Lightly, laughingly, she said, 'Well, I'm not usually popular with little girls!'

'And how many do you know?'

She didn't need to think about that. She shrugged, laughing again. 'None!'

They were only out for an hour or so, but it made a pleasant change, sitting in the gardens of a hotel where softly coloured lights lit the flowering bushes and palm trees. Scot talked to her about the islands, telling her about some caves he'd discovered which she might be interested to see.

They drove back to the villa at a leisurely pace under a star-studded sky in which a half-moon was suspended. The moon appeared to be bigger in this part of the world, Helen had noticed, bigger and golden.

As she got out of the car she remarked on the sweet, heady perfume of the flowers in the garden at the back of the villa, a perfume which wasn't there during daylight. 'I'm going to take some indoors,' she said eagerly. 'Scot, will you go in and bring me a pair of scissors?'

He hooked his jacket over his shoulder, laughing at her. 'Women! What a time to collect flowers! Okay, okay!'

Helen ventured deeper in to the garden as he went indoors—she could see well enough by the lights from the house. A moment later Lizzy emerged and bade her goodnight as she headed for her own house.

Helen waited patiently for the scissors. Where had Scot got to? She moved a little closer to the house and just as she did so she felt a tingling sensation in her feet. She glanced down at them—and screamed in horror. Her feet were covered with ants! They were black with them, millions of them, tiny scurrying creatures covering her feet!

'Scot!' Panic-stricken, she screamed his name.

He came running towards her as she bent, desperately trying to brush the ants away with her hands. She was obsessed, horrified at the idea of them running up her legs!

'Move!' he ordered.

She moved. She moved awkwardly closer to the light because she was still bending, still brushing frantically at her feet.

'Helen, I said *move*. You're standing on an ant's nest!'

Calmly he took hold of her arm and half dragged her from where she was standing, on to the gravel path which was fully illuminated. Within seconds he had cleared the little horrors from her feet and she stood there, shaking, letting him take over. He talked constantly as he brushed at her sandal-clad feet with his hands. 'Take it easy, they're just the regular variety! You'd have known about it if they'd been soldier ants.'

It was something of a consolation. As soon as the crisis was over she felt silly for reacting the way she had. But she also felt itchy, unclean. 'Oh, God, Scot, I'm sorry! Thank you, thank you. I—ugh! I've got to go and wash. *Now*.'

He roared with laughter. 'I'd have thought a brandy would do you more good.'

She couldn't see the funny side of it. All she could think about was washing, getting her tights off. 'That, too,' she said hastily. 'But I *must* take a shower. I'll join you in ten minutes.'

She felt cold inside. It might have been a typically feminine, even a stupid reaction, but she couldn't help it. It had been such a shock.

She showered quickly but thoroughly, still seeing in her mind's eye the blackness of the masses of ants on her feet. Certainly she had seen ants around the place, but only the odd straggler! Never in her life had she seen them in such numbers. Nor did she want to ever again, not on her person at any rate!

She threw her tights in the washbasin and filled it with hot water. It was crazy to be wearing tights in this weather, she knew, but the lower half of her legs had not been exposed to the sun and she had no choice but to wear tights when she was wearing a skirt.

She looked down at her two-tone legs, failing utterly to see the funny side of things. She leaned her head against the coolness of the bathroom mirror, suddenly drained of the confidence which had seemed of late to be returning to her.

'You're pathetic,' she said to her reflection. 'You've even lost your sense of humour.'

'Helen?' Scot's voice shattered the silence.

She went into her bedroom and called to him through

the door. 'I—Scot, I think I'll call it a night.' She
remembered his saying he wanted to make an early start
on the yacht. 'See you tomorrow, eight o'clock sharp.'
There were tears prickling at the back of her eyes and
she wished fervently she had not made a promise to
Samantha. The idea of going out on the yacht had lost
its sparkle.

There was no acknowledgment from Scot. 'Are you
there, Scot?'

'Open the door.' His voice was low, deadly serious.

'No, I think——'

'Open the door!'

She sighed, looking around for her robe. 'Just a
minute.'

He was leaning against the door frame, his hands
thrust inside the pockets of his slacks. 'What's wrong?
You said ten . . .' His eyes took in her state of undress.
'Hey, that really upset you, didn't it?'

'Yes. No. I—I'm just tired, that's all.'

His look searched the blue depths of her eyes until
Helen broke the contact and looked down at the floor.

'If you say so,' he said quietly, his hands reaching out
to cup her face, 'then I'll say goodnight.' He moved
closer to her, his lips brushing lightly over hers before
coming back to linger in a kiss which was almost chaste
and yet deliciously sensual.

She stiffened, moving easily out of his embrace.
'Scot!' The surprise was obvious in her voice as she
looked up at him, trying to assimilate what was
happening. How was she supposed to interpret *this*?

But she didn't have time to make an interpretation.
Scot's arms came tightly around her and his mouth
came down on hers and this time he was kissing her in
earnest. Every pulse, every nerve in her body leapt into
life as her lips parted beneath his and she forgot
everything—who she was and where she was. But that
reaction was shortlived. As Scot's hands moved over
her breasts, her brain started functioning and she put
on this the only interpretation there could possibly be.

She pulled away from him sharply, her hand flying

up to slap his face with a viciousness she would never have believed herself capable of.

He didn't move. He didn't blink. He looked stunned. 'My, my,' he said quietly. 'We certainly overreact to things, don't we?'

'Do we?' Her voice was full of sarcasm. She had been stupid enough to think that a friendship was growing between them. A *friendship*! But he had been planning *this* for days. 'You're a smooth operator, Scot, I'll give you that! Those dinners on the terrace, the drinks in the gardens tonight—all of which were instigated by you!' She glared at him, furious. 'And the way you've been coaxing me into conversation over the past several days, getting me to trust you, encouraging me to talk—it was all part of a seduction routine!'

'You're wrong——'

'Like hell I'm wrong!'

'Grow up!' he exploded. He grabbed hold of her roughly, his fingers bruising the flesh of her arms while he shook her as if she were a naughty child. 'Now you listen to me!' He let go of her, his eyes cold with anger. 'I've had more women than I care to remember, and at this stage in my life I do not go in for long and elaborate seduction routines! You're a beautiful girl—but don't flatter yourself. What happened just now was spontaneous. You gave me your answer and I accept it. But you only needed to say no. Hasn't anyone ever told you that you can't blame a man for trying?'

'Ordinarily, I wouldn't,' she spat. 'But in your case it's different. You're a married man, for heaven's sake! And I thought we—I thought we were just two people sharing a holiday villa and a temporary friendship. My God, am I naïve!'

Scot looked at her hard and long. 'Yes,' he said quietly. 'Yes, you certainly are.'

And then he was gone.

CHAPTER FOUR

HELEN sat down unsteadily in the cane chair by her dressing table. She had only herself to blame for all this. She had never stopped to think that by allowing Scot to get to know her a little she might be encouraging him.

Worse, she had not realised how attracted to him she was. Oh, she had acknowledged that he was a good-looking man, but she had made the acknowledgment detachedly, looking upon him simply as what he was—a stranger, one who happened to be male and very attractive with it.

But she had not been as detached as she'd thought. She had enjoyed his kissing her. No, no, she must be honest with herself—she had responded to it, she had loved it! For those few moments she had been tinglingly, deliciously *alive* for the first time in a long time, and in a way that she had never felt before.

She frowned, staring at an invisible spot on the wall as she searched her memory for a vague thought she had had during the night she spent with Corinne Clayman. She remembered thinking that if Corinne had been a man things would never have turned out the way they did. Whether she was in a mental fog or not, had Corinne been male she would not have dreamt of spending the night in that hotel suite, no matter how distressed she'd been.

Yet she had agreed to share a house with Scot for three or four weeks. What *had* she been thinking about? You can't blame a man for trying, he'd said. No, in the circumstances maybe she couldn't.

Regardless of what he'd said, Helen knew full well that she was not beautiful. But she was attractive, so why had she assumed he would be immune—married or not? It was obvious his marriage was not a good one—

where was his wife? Why wasn't she holidaying with her husband and daughter?

She took off her robe and got into bed, angry with herself. A minute later she sat up again and switched on the light. She was being too hard on herself. *He* was to blame, not she. There were so many factors which had made her sharing the house with Scot seem perfectly harmless. Firstly they were not alone; Samantha was there, and there were servants around all day. Secondly he was married, and he had made it crystal clear to Helen that he wanted to keep his distance from her, which was what she had wanted, too. And thirdly, Lizzy had said that on his visits here in the past Scot had been alone.

This third point had told Helen that the villa was not a place Scot used in which to conduct extra-marital affairs. Moreover, it had dispelled the vague suspicion she'd had that Corinne Clayman might be his mistress. Corinne was obviously just a friend of the family.

But really, all of these things had been hardly more than impressions on Helen's consciousness, impressions which had left her feeling at ease with the situation. Until now, she had not actually taken the trouble to analyse the information piece by piece.

And now that she had? Now what?

She switched the light off, thinking that tomorrow was going to be very, very awkward. She doubted very much whether she could find it in her heart to break the promise she had made to Samantha. Not only was she growing fond of the child, she also felt sorry for her, for reasons she couldn't explain.

That thought pulled her up short.

Tonight she had experienced so many emotions! She had known pleasure, fear, panic, anger. Somehow, at some point during these days with Scot she had started to feel again, to *care* about things.

It was quite a while before Helen slept, and she didn't sleep for long. She had a very bad night. Her own wretched cries woke her up and she spent the following hours tossing and turning, sweating, drifting in and out of sleep that was crowded with horrible dreams, dreams which were far removed from Trinini Island.

She got up at daybreak. In an effort to bring herself alive she took a cold shower, then she pulled on a pair of denims and a tee-shirt. Strangely enough she felt ravenously hungry. She felt as though she had spent the entire night going through a series of gruelling physical exercises. Maybe that accounted for her sudden appetite?

The house was silent. In the kitchen she moved deftly and quietly, putting together a cooked breakfast which she ate at the table in the dining area. She had just put her knife and fork down when Scot appeared.

He hadn't come downstairs; he'd come in from the beach. He was drying himself off with a towel as he walked in and when he spotted Helen, he threw it angrily to the floor. 'I want to talk to you,' he said abruptly.

He was as good as naked in brief white swimming trunks which left nothing to the imagination. His bronzed body was magnificent, still partially wet from his swim, the moisture curling the hair on his chest.

Helen looked away from him as he sat down at the table, his fingers raking the mane of hair back from his forehead. The sight of him disturbed her as much as his anger.

'I've had a sleepless night, thanks to you,' he began. 'And I'm damned if I'm going to apologise for finding you desirable!'

'Nobody's asking you to.'

He hesitated. Her remark seemed to have taken the wind out of his sails. 'Helen, I've never met anyone quite like you before.' He broke off, sighing. 'At least, not for many, many years. There are times when you're unbelievably shy and times when you're as forthright and blunt as—whatever. I've come to the conclusion that basically you're an old-fashioned girl. You've made it plain that you don't want our—er—relationship to progress any further, and I'll accept that. But if you deny there's a strong attraction between us, you're being dishonest.'

Their eyes met. Helen's denial stuck in her throat. Twelve hours ago she could have denied it and meant it, but she couldn't deny it now. Not since he'd kissed her.

'Well?'

She wasn't going to answer him. 'I don't see the relevance of this, Scot. I've asked nothing of you, nothing at all. We made an agreement, but somehow ... somehow you managed to forget it.'

'And you think I did that because I decided to seduce you,' he stated flatly. 'Well, you're wrong. I like you, Helen. I didn't come to the Bahamas looking for an affair any more than you did. ... Is there any coffee in that pot?'

She got up, glad of a temporary respite. 'I'll get you a cup.' By the time she came back from the kitchen, she had made a decision. 'I'm not going to leave the villa, Scot—I don't see why I should. So the best thing is for us to revert to our agreement and keep out of each other's way. Needless to say I shan't be coming with you on the yacht today.'

As she plonked the cup and saucer on the table he grabbed hold of her wrist and forced her back into the chair. 'You *will* be coming with us today! You're not going to let Samantha down.' He let go of her. 'Besides, you don't want to do that. You've got a soft heart, Helen. And that's one of the things I like about you.'

She was rubbing at her wrist. 'Now who's overreacting? And what would you know about people with soft hearts? You're as hard as nails!'

She didn't mean it. She didn't honestly think that about him. But she was having difficulty in forming an opinion of him. How could she, when he wouldn't tell her anything about himself?

Scot was shaking his head wearily. 'I'm not married, Helen. Does that change anything? I divorced Samantha's mother when Sam was one year old. I'm as free as the breeze.'

'You're free to make passes at whomever you please.' Her wryness did not detract from the truth of the statement, she realised.

'Absolutely. And why the sarcasm?'

'Because you're not free to get fresh with me, okay? If we can agree on that,' she sighed, 'then maybe we'll get on better.'

He grinned. It was as if he couldn't help himself. 'I've already agreed, remember?'

'I don't see what's funny——'

'Don't you, Helen? Don't you, really?' His eyes were dancing with laughter now. 'Then you'd better go and take a look at yourself in a mirror—a full-length mirror. When you spoke about friendship last night, I thought it was the funniest thing I'd heard in years. Especially when I realised you meant it. But I'm agreeable,' he added quickly. 'No more passes.'

He was still amused by what he was saying, but Helen was not. 'I have two questions for you, Scot, and if you're not prepared to answer them, you can go to hell.'

'Fire away.' He was still suppressing laughter.

'What is your full name, your *real* name?'

'Marcus Scot.'

'And is that supposed to mean something to me? Should I be impressed? I've assumed all along that you're someone in the public eye. I assumed that because you thought you'd been "tracked" to this island by someone who wanted to talk to you. I remember your remark, "Why can't you people leave me alone?" So you're either a murderer or someone who works on television.'

Damn the man, he was laughing openly now. 'I'm not a murderer. What's your second question?'

'Is Corinne Clayman your mistress?'

The laughter faded and was replaced by a frown. 'Now why should you think that?'

'Just answer me.'

'Did she mention me to you?'

'Certainly not. But you use her villa as your second home. And Corinne is a very beautiful woman.'

'So?' he drawled.

'So you won't answer me.'

There was no laughter at all now, none whatsoever. 'My relationship with Corrie is based solely on business. Business and nothing else. She's my agent—she's been my agent for years.'

'So you're an entertainer.'

'Yes, I suppose that's a fair description. I'm a pianist.'

'A pianist?' Helen was really surprised. 'I—I know this is going to sound silly—but you don't look like a pianist.'

'What does a pianist look like?'

'I told you it would sound silly.' Her eyes moved over to the piano. 'I'd thought that was Corinne's.'

'Technically, it is. She had it shipped over for me years ago. I sometimes come here to work, you see.' He smiled, a sudden flash of white against the tan of his skin. 'And I use this place as a retreat, too, somewhere I can be guaranteed privacy. This house belonged originally to Corrie's husband. She may have told you she's a widow? He was twenty-nine years older than she and a very wealthy man—an independent film producer whose second love was sailing around these cays.'

Helen was running his name through her mind. Marcus Scot. Marcus Scot . . . She turned her hands palms upwards, shrugging. 'I don't know why you've made such a mystery out of this,' she said reasonably, honestly. 'You might be well known in America, but you're not known in Britain. I'm afraid I've never even heard of you.'

'Good,' he said quietly. 'I'm glad about that, because I don't want you to think of me in association with anything. I want you to think of me merely as a man.'

Helen found herself almost mesmerised by his eyes. They were troubled, very serious. She felt disturbed by what she saw and she realised she ought to change the subject now, to lighten the atmosphere.

So she forced herself to laugh a little, wagging a finger at him. 'As a friend, Scot! I'll think of you as a temporary friend.'

'That'll do,' he agreed, smiling. 'Now, will you wake Samantha while I take a shower?'

It was a memorable day, a glorious, golden unforgettable day. Helen had never been on board a yacht before, and Scot explained a few things about it to her as they set sail.

He had named it *Lady Love*. It had been built in Florida and its overall length was thirty-one feet, but he spoke of it in terms of it being 'small' and 'nippy', saying that its shallow draught gave manoeuvrability, easy access to the beaches and coves in the area. He spoke to her of chains and warps, tenders and boat hooks, alcohol stoves and charcoal water filters, but most of this was lost on Helen. All she knew was that it was a gorgeous boat—a remark which amused Scot no end when she made it!

She was introduced to the crew, the two smiling young men who had trooped into the villa with suitcases and cartons on the day of the invasion. Lloyd was also on board, and he stood at the bows of the boat, watching out for the coral reefs—which were easily visible because the water was so clear.

Clear? The water around the islands was like liquid crystal, reflecting the deep, deep blue of the sky and glinting in the golden light of the sun! They sailed at a leisurely pace, going firstly around Trinini Island so that Helen could see aspects of it she had never seen before. The island was surrounded by beautiful beaches, beyond which were coconut groves and palmettos and fig trees.

They steered off towards the small cays to the northwest and Helen soaked up the sights, the silence and the pure sea air.

During the late morning, as the sun rose higher in the sky, Scot teased her because she was still fully dressed. He and Sam were in swimwear, but Helen had been so occupied with all she was seeing that she hadn't given a thought to her suntan.

'Come on, strip off! How much longer do I have to

wait?' The green eyes twinkled roguishly. 'You put your bikini on under that lot, didn't you? Before we left the villa?'

He sat back, his arms folded across his chest as he watched her deliberately. He succeeded in making her selfconscious and she pulled a face at him as she took off her slacks and tee-shirt. 'Stop that, you villain! You've seen it all before, anyhow.'

He muttered something which was deliberately indiscernible, glancing round to see whether his daughter was in earshot. She wasn't; she was standing at the bows with Lloyd, chattering away.

'I didn't quite catch that,' Helen grinned.

'I said——' And then he was laughing, deep, rumbling laughter which communicated itself to her.

'I know I look ridiculous!' she protested. 'But I've got this problem.'

Scot leaned closer to her as she sat down. 'My dear Helen, I'll admit that I find the sight incredibly sexy—knee-length socks teamed with an itsy-bitsy black bikini. But I happen to know you're not dressed like that for my benefit, so——'

She poked him in the ribs and pushed her socks down. 'Look, surely you've noticed . . .'

His eyes moved to her lower legs. 'Noticed what? Unfortunately I've never been close enough to——'

'Will you be serious for a moment? You're hopeless. Look—what do you make of this?'

He caught hold of her ankle, turning her leg so he could see the inner calf. He studied it for quite a time, serious now. 'Nothing,' he said at length. 'I'd say this is caused by stress.'

She looked at him quickly. 'That's what my doctor said, he said it's psychosomatic. But how did you know?'

His sweeping but comprehensive look was in no way suggestive. 'For one thing, you're obviously physically healthy, for another, I spent two years in medical school before I decided on a very different career. And of course I'm aware that you're deeply troubled, that you're bottling something up which must take its toll somehow or other. I heard you thrashing about in your sleep last night, Helen. Again.'

He pointed to her legs. 'Don't wear those socks again, let the air get to your legs. The sun won't do any harm at all, don't worry about that. Helen, stress affects different people in different ways. It's the cause of a myriad physical ailments which started out as psychosomatic pains. And some people get rashes, some have heart attacks, while others . . .' Something changed in his eyes and he glanced away for a second. 'Some people turn to drink.' He smiled, moving his arms in an expansive gesture. 'Speaking of which—what can I get you?'

'Do you know what I'd really like? A cup of tea.'

Scot got to his feet, looking at her as if she were mad. 'I should have known,' he said drily. 'What else would an Englishwoman want at this time of day? It'll be five minutes.'

Helen laughed softly as he went below deck. But her laughter quickly faded as her eyes lingered on his back before he moved out of sight. She closed her eyes. His attractiveness went beyond the physical. She had just seen yet another side of Marcus Scot, yet another of the moods of the man. And she had liked what she'd seen— yet again.

They had a picnic with wine and fresh fruit on the silky white sands of a tiny, deserted cove. The yacht's tender, as Helen discovered, was a small motorised boat, and this was what they used to reach the shore, leaving Lloyd and the other men on board the yacht.

Helen packed away the remains of their picnic in the cold box, declining Samantha's invitation to swim with her.

'Later, darling,' she explained. 'I'm too full at the moment, and it isn't good to swim when you're too full.' And when you've had several glasses of wine, she added to herself, suppressing a giggle.

'*I'm* not too full!' Sam protested, hopping towards the sea on one leg. 'Come in when you're empty, then, Helen!'

Scot was lying on his back on a beach towel. He opened one eye and peered at Helen. 'Charming turn of phrase, my daughter has. When you're empty!' He grunted and turned over.

Helen lay back, almost pinching herself to make sure she was really awake. The day, the setting, was gorgeous. So was the company. Her eyes seemed to move of their own volition to the man by her side. If he had been the world's worst father, which was no doubt a gross exaggeration, he was certainly making up for it now. Samantha was blooming, a happy little girl who was very different from the pale-faced child Helen had first set eyes on.

She watched the play of muscle in Scot's shoulders as he shifted his position slightly, knowing a sudden urge to run her fingers along the length of his back, to feel the smoothness of skin which was tanned a deep, golden brown. His hair had been bleached a shade lighter and she looked at the blondness of it, experiencing again an urge to touch.

Determinedly she turned her attention elsewhere and watched Samantha splashing about and then swimming. The child swam like a fish, dipping and diving and laughing to herself.

Scot's deep, resonant voice broke the silence. 'Are you in danger of falling asleep?'

'No. I'm keeping an eye on Sam, so don't worry, you sleep if you want to.'

'I wasn't thinking about that. I shan't sleep.' He turned over, reaching out to run his fingers along her arm. 'I'd better put some cream on you. You'll have to take it easy with those choc-ice legs until they catch up with the rest of you.'

It gave her an opportunity to laugh without his knowing it was uncomfortable laughter. She didn't want him to put cream on her. 'I can manage, thanks.'

He said nothing. He sat up and just watched her as she smoothed suncream on her legs and her arms and her front. When she'd finished, he said, 'I'll do your back for you.'

'That's okay,' she said lightly. 'I don't need any on my back, I'm lying on it.'

He shrugged and lay down again.

There came, of course, a time when Helen had to turn over, when the tropical sun at its meridian would not allow her to stay too long in one position. She did the best she could with the suncream, but it wasn't very satisfactory, and when the tube was taken from her hand she made no protest. To do so would have made all too obvious her misgivings.

Scot was not particularly gentle, and Helen was thankful for that. He started at her ankles and covered skin she had already covered, but he was more liberal with the cream. When his fingers trespassed to the curve of her inner thigh, she bit her lip, grateful that he couldn't see her face.

From then on his touch was sensual, or so it seemed to Helen. Maybe he hadn't altered the pressure of his touch at all, maybe it was all in her mind? But oh, it felt good!

She felt the straps of her bikini being untied and she stiffened. 'What are you doing?'

Very quietly he said, 'You don't want strap marks, do you? Why don't you take the thing off? There's no one around.'

She almost turned round to look at him—almost. She remembered just in time and said, 'Damn!' He had already started laughing when she reminded him, 'You're here, aren't you?'

They both joined Samantha in the sea eventually, and Helen marvelled at the child's energy. As soon as they boarded the yacht, however, Samantha was taken below deck by her father and put to bed. She slept all the way home.

Helen retreated to her room when they got back to the villa and Scot went upstairs for a shower, leaving Lizzy to feed Sam. She toyed with the idea of writing to Howard, then dismissed it. How could she begin to explain to him in a letter all that had happened to her, how she came to be in a private villa in the West Indies, of all places? No, all explanations and descriptions could wait until she next saw her brother.

She took a long and leisurely bath and washed her hair, letting it dry naturally before brushing it until it shone.

Her lower legs had caught the sun already, she noted with satisfaction. She wouldn't wear tights tonight. She had a long skirt with her, a flimsy thing in fine pink cotton which teamed with a halter-neck top.

Her dinner that evening with Scot made the perfect end to a perfect day, and she took care to thank him for it. 'It's been a wonderful day, Scot, thank you.'

He looked pleased. 'Even if it started out badly.'

Helen had forgotten their fight during the early morning. She had to think for a moment before she realised what he meant.

'The day isn't over yet,' he reminded her. 'I thought we might live dangerously after dinner . . .'

'What do you mean?' She looked at him a little uncertainly.

'Well, Sam's got a compendium of games upstairs. I thought we might have a game of chequers.' His eyes were laughing at her.

'Why, Scot, that really is living dangerously! But if it's draughts you're referring to then yes, I'm game!'

He groaned at the pun and did one better. 'I wish you'd check yourself when making remarks like that.'

Helen would not be outdone. 'Men! Why do they always see things in black and white?'

'Helen, if you go on like this, I'll be *bored* stiff!'

They ended up laughing like a pair of teenagers during the following couple of hours. Scot put some Charleston music from the twenties on the hi-fi and brought drinks out to the moonlit terrace. They played games old and new, ludo, Snakes and Ladders, draughts and a computer game Helen couldn't get the hang of, much to her disgust and to Scot's amusement.

It was midnight when they retired to their rooms, and Helen was not only physically tired after her long day, she also felt peaceful. She was convinced she'd have a decent sleep and she never thought for one moment that the long, dark hours of the night would turn out the way they did . . .

CHAPTER FIVE

SOMEONE was shaking her. There was a light in the room and someone was shaking her and saying her name over and over.

She felt her breath jerking into her lungs in a series of little sobs and then warm, strong arms came around her naked body and held her tightly, tightly and comfortingly. Her breath expelled on a long and shuddering sigh and she blinked against the light as the deep voice repeated her name.

'Helen . . . Helen . . . what is it? What *is* it?'

She couldn't see him; she was still seeing flashes of the dream that haunted her. And she was too close to him to be able to see him. One hand was pressed tightly against her back and his other hand was entwined in her hair, holding her head against his shoulder.

She became aware of skin against skin, aware that her breasts were pressing against the hardness of his bare chest, and she tried to pull away.

But Scot held her tightly and his voice was hardly more than a whisper against her ear. 'It's all right, you're safe now. You're safe, Helen. Take it easy now.'

Then she was sobbing. All nakedness was forgotten as great heaving sobs shook her body and Scot continued to hold her tightly, his hand stroking her hair as he encouraged her to cry, to let it go.

How long they remained like that, she would never really know. It didn't matter. When the sobs began to subside, Scott held her at arm's length, his eyes anxious as he searched her face. 'Tell me about it. *Talk* about it.'

'I——' She was sniffing, looking around for her box of tissues.

Scott stood up and fished in his pocket for a hanky.

He was barefoot, wearing only a pair of faded denims which had seen better days, and his thick mane of hair was tousled and wild.

'Here.' He sat on the edge of her bed as she blew her nose noisily, his eyes belying the smile on his face.

Helen took a deep breath, trying hard to steady herself. 'How—how did you get in here?'

'I have keys to all the rooms,' he said simply. 'Helen . . . talk to me, please. Will you tell me about it?'

She wanted to say yes, but she couldn't speak. Her eyes closed as her vision blurred and his face went out of focus. So she nodded, reaching for the sheet as she became aware once again of her nakedness, aware that only the lower half of her body was covered.

His smile was sad as he stood up. 'Don't worry about that,' he said quietly. 'Here.' He handed her robe to her.

She swallowed against the fresh bout of tears, but it didn't help. They streamed down her face. 'If—if you'll just leave me alone a moment . . .'

'To hell with that,' he said gently. 'Come on.' He took hold of her shoulders as she got out of bed and she stood, like a little child, as he guided her arms into her robe.

And then he did something, just a small thing, which she knew she would remember for as long as she lived. He pulled her head gently against his shoulder and put his arms around her lightly, just lightly, satisfying himself that she was steady on her feet. In those few seconds, Helen felt herself relax and she had the craziest and most unrealistic thought: she thought she loved him.

'Come on.' Scot steered her towards the door. 'You will sit in the lounge and I'll make us some coffee.'

A small sound escaped from her, a cross between a sob and a sigh. She looked up at him, attempting what must have been a parody of a smile, and he pressed his lips against her forehead.

It was a while before she could speak coherently. She

started jerkily at the end of the story, by telling Scot when her father had died.

She cried again and again as she talked, silent tears, and Scot sat patiently by her side, not touching her in any way, knowing she would continue when she was able to. 'I—dropped out of university, and I'm glad. It was the best thing I ever did,' she babbled. 'Dad was disappointed and he never realised I'd only gone in the first place to please him. I was halfway towards a B.A., but—anyway, I came home to live and I had—I had the last two years with him, at least. But . . . Oh, God, Scot, I'm so *angry*! So very, very *angry*!'

Her hands tightened into fists and she held them against her mouth, doubling over as if in pain as she remembered . . . 'He—Dad was a Headmaster at a local school. One—night he went out to post some letters. He belonged to the local amateur dramatic society, and I used to help out sometimes, and that's where we'd been this night. We got home around eleven o'clock. We'd—been for a drink with a few . . . We started talking about the evening's events when we got home and—and I was on my way to bed when he said he was going out to post some letters. They were on his desk in his study. They were something to do with his school and . . . and it wasn't unusual for him to go out late to post letters. The pillarbox was only a ten-minute walk away, for God's sake. *For God's sake!*'

She got up, moving around restlessly. There was a bottle of bourbon on the bar and she helped herself to some, swallowing the liquid without tasting it before she went on. 'It was only when I came out of the bathroom and got undressed that I realised Dad hadn't come back. I thought nothing of it.'

Helen closed her eyes, telling the next part in a stream of words which peppered rapidly from her lips because that was the only way she could get through it. 'I got into bed and I switched off my light, but I was listening for his key in the door. The sound never came and I thought he'd gone for a walk, then I thought, no, he'd have said so if he was going to do that. Half an hour must have passed by then and I got out of bed and flung some clothes on because I suddenly got this awful feeling in the pit of my stomach. I grabbed my house key and went downstairs, and when I opened the front door, my father was there, half—half kneeling, half standing on the doorstep. He was trying to reach the doorbell. That was what I found when I opened the door, and Dad looked up at me and his face was covered in blood, and I keep . . . and I keep . . .'

Scot moved rapidly to her side, but she did not break down. She put her cold hands in to the warmth of his hands and he said, 'Say it, Helen, say it.'

'And I keep dreaming about it. Just that one picture, that one, awful moment. I dream about it night after night. He—I—I could hardly see his features for the blood streaming from a gash on his head. He'd almost crawled back to the house and—and nobody had seen him. He'd been mugged, Scot. He'd been mugged and robbed of the contents of his pockets. And do you know what they were? Do you *know*?' Her voice rose hysterically. 'One pen, one cheque book, one credit card and thirteen pounds in cash. *Thirteen pounds*. They *killed* him for thirteen pounds!'

Scot swore viciously, and Helen repeated what he'd said word for word, matching the violence in his voice. 'He'd only gone out to post some letters . . .'

'Easy now.' The grasp of his hands tightened almost painfully. 'Come and sit down.'

They sat down and Scot waited for a moment before pressing her to go further. 'You said they killed him. The blow to his head was fatal?'

'No, it wasn't that. But they killed him, all right. *They* killed him!' Her voice was dull, lifeless. 'I got him into a chair and phoned the ambulance immediately, and while I was speaking on the phone, he had a heart attack. I saw it happening. I saw him—his face was . . . I'll never forget how he looked. And I was helpless.'

'But the ambulance was on its way?'

'Yes. Yes, and he survived. It was a massive heart attack, but he survived it.' She drew a long, shuddering breath, taking strength from the pressure of Scot's hands around hers. 'There followed five weeks which—which are almost dream-like to me now, though I was all right then. I stayed off work for a few days then I went back and I was—okay. My brother had come down to stay for a few days and when it got near Christmas, he came back again for the holidays.

'I went to the hospital every night and . . . he seemed to be getting better by the day, but . . . but he had a second heart attack in the early hours of Christmas morning and——'

'He was still in the hospital?'

'Yes. They did all they could, but it was hopeless. He died on Christmas Day.'

She lay back against the cushions of the settee, staring into space. At length Scot asked. 'Were they caught? The man or men who——'

'There were three of them—three youths. Yes. They're in prison now. But they weren't tried for murder!' She shot suddenly to her feet, her arms flailing angrily.

Scot was silent. He let her be, he let her go on and on, giving vent to the anger that had been eating away at her for so long.

'He wouldn't have died but for them!' Helen shouted at one point. 'He was fit and strong. He was—he was *not* a candidate for a heart attack!'

Time passed. Scot made fresh coffee and said only enough to encourage her to go on when necessary. At length she cried again, and when the tears finally subsided, he knew there would be no more for some time. She would cry again, but next time she would cry in private. She had, finally, started to mourn her father's death. He was privileged that she had opened up to him like this. He was privileged, trusted, and he appreciated that fact. More, perhaps, than she would ever know.

He moved closer to her. 'Helen,' he said softly, 'your story is tragic and there's little I can say to comfort you. The harsh reality is something you already know: there is nothing anyone can do, ever, to change the past. It's written. It's happened. It's gone.'

She had known it. Of course that was true. But there was something in the way Scot presented the truth, some ring of finality in his voice, which made her *absorb* the fact. 'Yes.'

'From now on that recurring dream will be less and less frequent. In time it will fade—I promise you that. And your father would be the first to rejoice at this, the start of your recovery.'

'Yes,' she whispered. 'Yes, he would. He wouldn't want——'

'Exactly. He wouldn't want his daughter to fall apart.' Scot stood and pulled her gently to her feet. 'Now go and bathe your eyes. There's something I want you to see.'

She did as he bade her, feeling as though an enormous weight had lifted from her shoulders. She washed her face in cold water and held two pads of wet cotton-wool against her eyes. Then she combed her hair and found that she had the presence of mind to cringe at her reflection in the mirror. She looked awful. But she would feel no selfconsciousness with Scot.

The image of his holding her naked body against him flashed through her mind. No, she would never again feel any selfconsciousness with Scot.

She remembered, too, the thought she had had earlier. She still felt that way about him. But it would all seem different in the morning. Tomorrow she would, she felt sure, accept the fact that she was confusing love with gratitude.

How kind he had been to her! And there had been times, during their first few days together, that she had thought there was no depth to the man.

But it was already morning, she realised as she found Scot waiting outside her bedroom door. He took her arm and led her along the terrace to the back of the villa, which faced due east. She had watched many times the sun sinking into the sea at the front of the house, but this morning she stood with Scot's arm around her shoulder and watched the sunrise. The dawn of a new day.

'It's funny,' she said to him, 'I've been so—so much better these last few days. I'd honestly believed I *was* better, over it. But it's only now that I feel freed, released from— I don't know how to describe it.'

'Then don't try,' he smiled. 'Because I understand exactly what you mean.'

'I don't know how to thank you, Scot.'

'There's no——' He broke off, a look of pleasure on his face as he saw that she had found a way to thank him.

Helen slipped her arms around his neck and kissed him.

CHAPTER SIX

IT was almost three in the afternoon when she woke up. 'Disgraceful!' It was the first word out of her mouth as she leapt out of bed, thinking about all the sun she had missed. She went into the bathroom, muttering to herself.

Still, it had been very late—or very early—when she'd gone to bed. She wondered whether Scot would be up yet. He hadn't gone to bed when she had; he'd been pouring himself a drink when she'd said goodnight.

She slipped into a pair of shorts and a bikini top, brushed her hair and was gratified to see that her eyes were back to normal. She felt good. She had slept like a log. She looked out of the window to see whether there was any sign of Scot and Sam on the beach. The beach was empty. But the yacht was there, so they hadn't gone out for the day.

She was pleased by that. No, she was not in love with Scot. In the cold light of day, she realised that what she felt for him was gratitude. Of course she liked him very much, too—but that was a different thing entirely.

He was reading a book in the living room. 'Ah, so there you are!'

'Good morning! Where is everyone?'

'It's Sunday. Lizzy and Lloyd have gone to see their children, which really means they've gone to see their grandchildren, and they've taken Sam with them. Well, she asked Lizzy if she could go, to tell you the truth! Little madam. When I told her you'd be sleeping most of the day and that I wasn't taking her out to mess about on the boat, she tagged on to Lizzy!'

'But Lizzy didn't mind?'

'She was delighted.'

Helen was heading for the kitchen when all he'd said registered with her. 'Grandchildren? I didn't know

79

Lizzy had any children, let alone grandchildren. She—they don't look old enough to have grandchildren, do they?'

'They start young over here,' he called to her. 'I'll have some coffee if you're about to make some, Helen.'

'Have you had lunch?' she asked.

'No. I've just told you, Lizzy's out for the day.'

Helen poked her head round the kitchen door. 'Dear me! Are you one of those men who doesn't know how to boil an egg?'

Scot looked at her blankly. 'What's an egg?'

She was only too happy to cook for him, only too happy to feed him. They started with a chunk of melon, followed by a Spanish omelette, followed by ice cream.

'Incredible!' Scot leaned back contentedly. 'Where did you conjure all that from?'

She cocked an eyebrow at him. 'I looked in the fridge. She laughed at him. 'It wasn't exactly exotic, but I do have a gift for——'

'Oh, Helen!' Scot tapped himself on the forehead. 'Speaking of gifts—you've just reminded me. It's Sam's birthday tomorrow. Will you come into town with me and help me choose something for her?'

'Certainly.' She was just starting to clear the table when Scot let out another exclamation.

'Hell! Lizzy and Lloyd have taken the car!'

Helen went into the kitchen. 'So what's wrong with your legs?'

She wasn't aware that he'd followed her until his arms slid around her from behind. She plonked the dishes on the draining board before she dropped them.

He was holding his hands together in front of her waist, imprisoning her. 'There's nothing wrong with my legs, you devil. But it's quite a walk. Are you up to it?' Then loosening his hold so she could turn to face him, 'Seriously, Helen?'

'I'm fine.' She looked in to his eyes. 'Really, I'm fine. Thanks to you.'

He brushed his lips against her temple, sending a shiver of pleasure down her spine. 'You thanked me last night,' he whispered. Looking down at her, he added more loudly, 'At least I think you did. I didn't quite hear what you said, though.'

Helen tried and failed to suppress a smile. 'Is that so?' But she was not about to give a repeat performance. Last night had been a very emotional time for her, but there was no way she was going to take the initiative with him now!

He kissed her. It was sweet and brief but delicious. 'Was that what you said?'

'I . . .' Helen's heartbeat had increased abominably. 'It was something like that.'

She honestly had not meant it as an invitation, but that was how Scot interpreted her uncertainty. 'Or did you say this?' He kissed her deeply, hungrily, tasting the warm softness of her mouth as her lips parted beneath his of their own volition.

This time her heartbeat quickened to a dizzying extent and her pulses started to throb in response to the feel of Scot's body against hers. She broke the contact while her ability to think straight still prevailed.

'No, Scot. I—I didn't say that much.'

His smile was wry. 'I had a feeling I'd read too much into it.'

She turned away and put the plates into the sink. 'What are we going to do for Sam's birthday?'

'Do?'

'Well, she'll be six years old tomorrow, Scot. Surely she'll expect something more than a present, won't she?'

He looked a little lost. He sighed, seeming cross with himself. 'You're right. If we were at home in L.A. she'd have a party. My housekeeper would—but what can we do out here?'

'We can get Lizzy to bake a cake for her. We can have tea in the afternoon, asking Lizzy and Lloyd to join us. And the boys from the boat. We can adapt, can't we? Play games or musical chairs or something. Use your imagination!'

He was nodding, a strange smile playing around his lips. 'I'm pretty hopeless, aren't I?'

'No,' she said kindly. 'And you're getting better by the day, Scot. Honestly you are.'

She could not interpret the look in his eyes. Their eyes met and held for long seconds, but she could not begin to guess what was in his mind.

They walked to the shops, but it was in the market that they found presents suitable for a six-year-old. There wasn't a great deal to choose from, not for a sophisticated little girl who clearly had everything she could want materially. Helen boughts gift, too—a doll and a beach ball, and Scot bought her a couple of dresses and a colourful spinning top which was just like a toy Helen had played with when she was Sam's age.

Over dinner she remembered something Samantha had said days ago. 'Didn't Sam say something about you visiting England after you've been to Disneyland? Are you taking her anywhere else in Europe?'

'No, no, you've got it all wrong, Helen. Sam won't be coming with me to England. I'll only be in the country for one or two nights. One, probably. Samantha was talking about when we emigrate. That's when she's going to England—permanently.'

'*Emigrate?* You mean you're going to live in England?'

'Why are you so surprised? That's where I was born, after all.'

'Yes, but——' Helen picked up her wine glass, not wanting him to guess at the other things she was feeling. He had already remarked on her surprise. But the news had been more than that, it had been a shock; and furthermore, her very first thought was that she might see Scot again. That maybe the end of this holiday would not be the end of their relationship. And the idea of that gave her pleasure, so much that she wanted to hide it from him.

Casually, she asked, 'Are you hoping—intending to make a name for yourself in Britain? Professionally, I mean.'

'I know what you mean.' He seemed vaguely amused.

'No, that is not my intention, my reason for emigrating. I'm going home to roost, if you like. I want——'

Helen found the amusement in his eyes offputting. 'You don't need to explain anything to me, Scot.'

'I know I don't need to.' The amusement vanished instantly. 'But I want to. You see, I'm about to make a lot of changes in my life, my lifestyle. Corinne is over there looking for a house for me.'

Helen sipped at her wine, knowing a sense of disappointment. He had said that his relationship with Corinne was purely one of business. Was it or wasn't it?

'... Among other things,' he went on. 'She's also hunting for antiques—her favourite hobby. And no doubt she's on a regular shopping spree, too, as was your impression.'

She put her question lightly. 'Corinne's emigrating, too, is she?'

'No, no,' he said quickly. 'She's house-hunting for me simply because I don't have the time to do it. That is, I didn't have time for house-hunting as well as taking a vacation. And this vacation with Sam was far more urgent, far more important.'

He lit a cigarette, shrugging. 'Corrie will never leave America. It suits her down to the ground.'

Quite what that meant, Helen had no way of knowing. She knew only that if there were something more than business between Scot and Corinne Clayman, it couldn't be too serious if he was about to emigrate and she was staying in America.

Almost to himself he added, 'Corrie's very much a career-woman. She likes making money, though God knows she doesn't need to make more. She's been a good friend to me, a damn good agent, too. Ah, yes, she's very business-orientated. A formidable lady when she's crossed ...'

'Formidable? That's the last word I'd have used to describe her! She's warm and generous and——'

'Oh, yes,' Scot conceded, 'that, too. All in all, she's quite a character.'

'She'll—continue working for you? Will she try to find you work in England?'

There was that funny smile again. 'No. When I leave the U.S.A. in the fall, it will be the parting of the ways for me and Corrie.'

Helen was glad to hear it. But what difference would it make to her? What *was* she thinking about? Scot had given no hint that he wanted to see her again in England, and he'd had plenty of opportunity to do so.

'So you're emigrating in the autumn.'

'Or early winter.' He shrugged. 'I have several commitments to fulfil before I can move. My hands are tied. I've got a lot of work ahead of me. I shouldn't really be taking this time off to——' He looked at her quickly. 'Helen, have you ever been to America?'

'Yes. I spent three days in New York with my boss last year.'

Scot's eyebrows went up. 'Oh, yes?' he drawled.

'Oh, *no*. I was with my boss and his *wife*. It was strictly business.'

'Is there a man in your life?'

'Only my brother.' She smiled sadly.

'Sorry. I meant——'

'I know what you meant, Scot. No, there isn't.'

'What—where was I? Oh, yes. I was checking that you've got a visa for the States.'

'Of course. Have you forgotten that I came here via Florida?'

'Yes, I had. Look, I don't suppose you'd consider ...' He looked at her doubtfully. 'I don't suppose you'd consider coming to Disneyland for a few days? You see, I've promised Sam and there's no way I can get out of it. Would you?'

Would she consider going to Disneyland? Certainly she would! She was by no means too old to find the sparkle and fun of Disneyland, a place she'd heard so much about, uninviting. She had been told by several adults that they had enjoyed the place as much as their children had.

If only ... 'When are you going?'

'In a couple of weeks, when we leave here.'

'Oh. No, I can't, Scot.' It was depressing to realise she had already been on Trinini Island for two weeks. She had to consider Geoff Mortimer, he'd been kind to her, and to take more than a month off work would be unfair.

Scot pushed his chair from the table and stretched out his legs. 'I didn't think it would appeal to you.'

'Oh, but it does! Very much so! I—it's just that I daren't take more than a month off work. My boss——'

Scot seemed delighted. 'Is that your only reason?'

'Of course.'

'You would be my guest, you understand.'

She smiled. 'I'm not worried about the expense, either. I have savings I haven't even dipped into for this holiday.'

'*My guest*,' he repeated. 'So, that's great! We'll stay here just one more week, then. That will give us a couple of days' travelling time to L.A. and a few days in Walt's wonderland. I'll see that you're on a plane back to the U.K. to get you back to work in time. ... Wait a minute, wait a minute, I've got a better idea.'

'Go on.'

'We won't go to Disneyland, we'll go to Disney World.'

'I'm not sure of the difference,' Helen admitted.

'The first is in California, the second is in Florida. And I'd be better off in Florida—much less likely to run into people I know.'

Helen frowned. 'You mean people who know you, don't you? Reporters?'

'Reporters,' he nodded. 'And the advantage to you will be a much shorter journey back to England if we settle for Florida. So is it settled?'

'It's settled,' Helen agreed. 'Tell me, isn't one of these places bigger than the other? I mean, there's more to see at one of them.'

'That's right. The one in Florida is the bigger.'

'Then it's definitely settled!'

Scot threw back his head and laughed. 'Why, Helen, you're just a great big kid at heart, mm?'

He went out there and then to make a phone call from the yacht club, saying he would get a friend to arrange accommodation for them.

Samantha was over the moon on hearing the news. She said that Helen's going with them to Disney World was her 'real' birthday present—which pleased Helen enormously. Her birthday tea was a tremendous success and was attended by Lizzy's grandchildren, whom Sam had met the previous day, one of whom was the same age as Sam. Helen played 'The Teddy Bears' Picnic' on the piano for the first round of Musical Chairs, and then Scot took over and played, very rapidly, the kind of piano music which used to accompany the old Keystone Cops silent movies.

This amused Helen, and everyone else, no end. She remembered her nonsensical remark that Scot didn't 'look' like a pianist. Actually, she still thought so. But he could certainly make the keyboard talk, there was no doubt about that.

The days moved on, complete and full and sunny. They were unforgettable days, days of laughter, yachting, swimming, snorkelling; Helen even tried her hand at sailboarding. There would never be a holiday which would equal this one, she knew. Because on her future holidays Scot would not be there. It was he who had made this time so perfect for her, he who made her think in terms of golden days and silver nights.

They would be sailing back to Florida this coming Sunday, and Helen was looking forward to seeing something of the State. So far she had seen only the airport at Miami. But she would be sorry to leave Trinini Island, much as she was looking forward to Disney World.

She said as much to Scot on the Thursday night. They were in the lounge, having a last drink before calling it a night. Since dinner they had been listening to music and drinking fairly steadily, feeling no need whatever to make conversation.

When Scot switched the hi-fi, off, Helen said, 'I'll be sorry to leave here on Sunday.'

'Trinini? Me, too. Can't say I'm looking forward to tramping around Disney World, even if you and Sam are!'

It was not at all what Helen had meant, but it was just as well he could not guess what was going through her mind. To her, their leaving the island was a marker in time, the day which signalled the reality that her holiday was coming to an end. . . . Which meant that her relationship with Scot was coming to an end. And it was. If he had been going to suggest that they meet again in England, he'd have done so by now. But he had not. He hadn't mentioned England at all since they'd talked about his emigration.

A momentary depression descended on her and she looked down at the Campari in her glass, thinking that maybe the alcohol was partially responsible for her feeling so blue. Was this her third drink or her fourth? . . . on top of the wine she'd had during dinner.

She chided herself; the drink had nothing to do with her feeling of depression. Who was she trying to fool? She was in love with Marcus Scot and gratitude had nothing whatever to do with it.

'Helen, where have you gone?'

'Oh—work,' she lied. 'I was think about work. That's what I meant when I said I'd be sorry to leave the island—it brings the prospect of work that much closer.'

'Don't you like working in the gallery?'

'I love it.' She groaned inwardly, aware that she seemed to be contradicting herself. 'But . . . you know, one is completely free when on holiday. I mean, there are no deadlines of any sort, no commuting.'

She got out of it nicely; her explanation made perfect sense to him. He was nodding in agreement, saying something about looking forward to the time when he would be free of commitments.

He was sprawled in the chair, his shoes on the floor, his feet on the edge of a coffee table. He was wearing a dark blue knitted shirt and the white slacks he'd worn the night she had first had a meal with him. That first dinner, an awkward, almost silent meal, seemed so very long ago now . . . and yet the intervening days had sped by.

Helen finished her drink and put her glass down, knowing she must go to her room before she said something she would regret, before she gave Scot a hint of how she really felt about him and thereby made a fool of herself.

'Would you like another drink?' He was standing over her now, motioning towards her empty glass.

'No. No, I'm off to bed.' She stood up, smiling, keeping her voice light. 'What time have I to set my clock for the morning?'

For a moment, he didn't answer her. He just looked at her, his beautiful, clear green eyes moving slowly over every inch of her face and her silky, shoulder-length hair. 'Seven. We'll go out at eight. Helen . . .' His hands were on her shoulders, moving slowly down the smooth skin of her arms until he was holding her hands in his. 'Have you any idea how much I want you? Have you any idea what it's been costing me to keep to that stupid agreement? To be a friend to you and nothing else?'

'Scot, I——'

She got no further. He pulled her arms around his back and claimed her lips with a passion that alarmed her. Within seconds she was returning his kiss, kissing him for all she was worth and encouraging his intimate exploration of her mouth. When his hands moved over her breasts, she moaned softly, her head going back in invitation as his lips trailed a path of fire along her throat, her neck.

'You want me,' he murmured. 'You want me, Helen . . .'

It would have been senseless to deny it, senseless to deny what her body was telling him only too clearly.

Yes, she wanted him, but in her mind and in her heart was the knowledge that this would be nothing more than a brief affair. For Scot, just one among many, no doubt.

'Scot, no! I don't want——'

'You want, my darling,' he whispered against her ear, his hands teasing, caressing, the fullness of her breasts. 'You want me as much as I want you. We'll make love all night long, Helen, we'll make up for lost time and . . .' His lips moved against the hollow at the base of her throat while his hands slid down to her hips, pulling her against the length of his body, leaving her in no doubt as to the passion and need within him.

'Oh, God!' With a cry she tore herself away from him, her trembling hands reaching for the buttons he had opened on her blouse.

'What is it?' Scot reached for her, cupping her face between his hands. 'Why deny. yourself? I don't understand why you should——'

'No,' she said quickly. 'No, Scot, I don't suppose you do.'

'Helen, we're free, we're adult and we want each other. Life is short, Helen, and if two——'

'Stop it!' He was touching her again, his thumbs moving in lazy circles over the aroused peaks of her breasts. He was touching her . . . and she was weakening by the second.

But she had heard similar words from a couple of boy-friends in the past, men whom it had been very easy to resist because she had not felt a corresponding need. Her need for Scot had taken her by storm, body and mind. But these *were* just lines he was giving her. Oh, he had much more panache, sophistication, expertise . . . but they were lines nevertheless.

She walked away from him without another word. She just walked away and prayed he would not follow her. She muttered goodnight in a voice which was full of emotion as she reached the door, but she did not look back.

It was her tone of voice, she knew, which prevented

him from pursuing her. She closed her bedroom door and leaned heavily against it, feeling that she had let herself down terribly. She had meant her goodnight to be snappy and curt, but it had not come out like that. It had come out in a strangled voice which must have told him she was on the brink of tears.

And what, she wondered desperately, would he make of that?

CHAPTER SEVEN

SHE needn't have worried. Scot had clearly mis-
understood the unhappiness in her voice, because
during breakfast the following morning he kept
glancing at her with concern in his eyes.

Helen had woken with a screaming headache and she
had told Scot and Samantha what was amiss as soon as
she set eyes on them. She would not be joining them on
the yacht today—she hadn't even bothered to dress.
Samantha offered to stay at the villa and 'look after'
her, but Helen explained that what she wanted most of
all was silence and a little more sleep.

'Go upstairs and get your things, honey,' Scot said to
his daughter. 'We'll be leaving in five minutes.'

As soon as the child was out of earshot, he turned
to Helen. 'It's your father, isn't it? You've been going
over it all again. And last night . . . I should have
realised.' He took hold of her hand, his eyes
narrowing as he examined her face. 'Did you have the
dream again?'

'No,' she said honestly. 'This headache is just . . .' She
shrugged, unsure what had caused it. 'Just tension, I
suppose.'

'Sexual,' Scot stated flatly, with a twinkle in his eye.
'It's a pity you didn't take the preventative.'

She tried not to laugh at him. 'Well, that's different! I
thought it was usually referred to as a cure for
headaches?'

'It's that, too. Prevention is better than cure, though.
Still, if you'd like me to stay around today, we can
always hand Samantha over to Lizzy for the
morning . . .'

'Get out of here!'

She was still giggling after he and Samantha had left,
when she got back into bed. It had occurred to her by

91

then that her headache could only be the result of one drink too many the previous night.

She closed her eyes, marvelling at the way she was so uninhibited with Scot, so unselfconscious and relaxed. What was it—how come he had such a gift for bringing her out the way he did? She didn't dare to think of how she would feel when he flew back to Los Angeles and she flew back to England.

'Don't spoil things,' she said to herself in the silence of her room. 'Don't spoil these last precious days with thoughts like that.'

She slept till noon. After the hearty lunch Lizzy produced, she was feeling fine. The headache had gone and she was wondering what to do with herself for the rest of the day. Already she was missing Scot's company and wishing she'd gone out on the yacht, headache or no. Still, perhaps it was as well he was having a day alone with his daughter; that was, after all, the reason he had come to the Bahamas.

And she? She had come here in the hope of sorting her life out, making plans for the future. But she still hadn't made a decision as to whether or not she would sell the house.

She stayed indoors and finished the last few pages of the book she had been reading. When that was done, she fished through a rack of records and put a Glenn Miller album on the hi-fi. It was the original recordings from the film, 'The Glen Miller Story', and she had a copy of it at home. It had been her father's. Anthony Good had loved music of all kinds and Helen was equally eclectic.

She pulled a Bing Crosby LP from the rack and moved on to the next rack. Corinne's record collection was terrific.

Then she remembered the unmarked cassettes she had seen and she wondered whether these might in fact belong to Scot. Maybe they were recordings of him playing the piano?

They were.

And Helen had never been as shocked by listening to music as she was when she played the first cassette.

There was a plain white label on its box on which there was written a date and a few scrawled words she couldn't make out. For the first few seconds of the tape there was silence, followed by a crackling noise, followed by a man's voice—Scot's voice—saying, 'Okay, Hal, take it from the top.'

Something was said in reply to this, something Helen couldn't catch, and was answered by Scot's voice, this time holding a ring of irritation. 'It's too slack, it's still too slack, Hal! Take it from the top . . .'

After another short silence the music began. The piano was only one among many instruments, a full orchestra. It stopped abruptly and Helen clicked her tongue in frustration, realising that this random tape she had picked was either part of a recording session or a rehearsal. The music stopped and started twice before the piece was played through to the end, the piano being dominant over the other instruments.

Helen's frown deepened as she listened. She knew the music well, very well. It was the theme from a film. She shot to her feet, staring stupidly, disbelievingly, at the hi-fi, because she also knew who had written the theme . . . and his name was *not* Marcus Scot.

She stabbed at the button on the hi-fi, ejected the tape and slipped another one in. No, there was no doubt about it, no mistake. By the time she had played twenty minutes of the cassette, she was in no doubt whatever about the true identity of Marcus Scot.

Several things, little things she had seen and heard recently, clicked into place, and her first reaction was one of anger at Scot's deceit. 'Oh, how very, very clever of him!' she muttered to the room. She stopped the tape. She didn't need to hear any more.

'What is your full name, your *real* name?' she had demanded of him. And he had told her. Oh yes, no doubt he had told her the truth in saying his real name was Marcus Scot. But that wasn't the name he was known by—it wasn't his *professional* name!

His professional name was Scot Montague, and while his face had not been familiar to her when she had first met him, she certainly knew the name. So would anyone else, in Britain, as well as the States—in Europe and on the far side of the world, too, for all she knew. Anyone who took the trouble to read the back of record sleeves, or listened to the radio, or watched television, or patronised the cinema would know the name. A pianist, indeed!

Scot Montague was a composer, songwriter, lyricist. His name occasionally appeared on T.V. in the credits of American programmes ... 'Music by Scot Montague'. He was an enormously talented man whose compositions appealed to all kinds of people, whose lyrics were sung by artists ranging from ballad singers to pop groups. He was not himself a singer, but he had had a hit record, an instrumental piece, in Britain about three years ago, in which he played the piano. It was the theme from a very popular and successful film. And the name of the theme was 'Lady Love'—which was also the name of his yacht.

Scot Montague was at the zenith of his career. The success of 'Lady Love' was just starting to happen for him all over again—with a difference. He had written the music for a new film, one which was currently on release in London. And this film had recently won that most glittering of Hollywood prizes for 'Best Film of the Year', and so had the composer of the theme music ... an Academy Award. An Oscar.

So *that* was who Oscar was!

Samantha had said Oscar belonged to Scot, and at the time Helen had assumed the mysterious Oscar to be a dog or an unwanted uncle or something! No wonder he hadn't wanted to bring it with him to Trinini. Whoever took a statue on holiday?

Helen sank into a chair, looking dazedly around the room. Oscar wasn't merely a statue; it was what it represented that mattered.

And she knew, now, what 'Minestrow' meant. It was the childish pronunciation of Maestro—a name by which Scot's close friends referred to him.

Maestro. Scot Montague—good heavens! Incredible.

And yet ... *why* hadn't she realised before now? She should have, she really should have.

Helen's anger had vanished. It was replaced by bewilderment. No, there was in fact no reason on earth why she should have known, why she should have recognised him. Scot's name was extremely well known, but his face was not. Why should she have recognised someone who had never, to her knowledge, appeared on British T.V., whose face never appeared in British newspapers?

He had been larking about on the piano on Sam's birthday; she would never have guessed from hearing that! She dropped her head into her hands, feeling idiotic as she remembered the way she had banged out 'The Teddy Bear's Picnic'.

She felt even more foolish when she remembered some of the things she had said to Scot when he'd been talking about emigrating: 'Are you hoping to make a name for yourself in Britain?' 'Will Corinne try and find you work over there?'

What a *joke*!

A joke on *her*.

Why hadn't he told her? Why on *earth* hadn't he told her who he really was?

'Because I don't want you to think of me in association with anything else,' he had said, when she'd told him she'd never heard of him.

Helen looked up, her eyes narrowing thoughtfully as she played this sentence, and its meaning, through her mind. That, and ... 'I want you to think of me merely as a man.'

To use Scot's own idiom, what was the big deal? Of *course* he was just a man, just a human being like everyone else. Helen was no worshipper of the famous. He could have told her, he *should* have told her.

Her emotions shifted again. She had gone from anger to bewilderment. She had felt foolish and then puzzled. And now she felt sad.

The sadness lasted as she sat there, mulling it all over. Scot had not told her because he didn't trust her, it was obvious. He had wanted to keep this information from her. Why? Because she might earn herself a fast buck by phoning the American press and letting them know where he was hiding out for some peace and privacy? Surely he couldn't think that of her!

No, he didn't think that of her. She was not so lacking in confidence that she could entertain that notion for long.

So why hadn't he trusted her? Helen thought about it and thought about it, but she couldn't come up with an answer.

She would tackle him about it tonight.

'I've missed you today.' These were the first words out of Scot's mouth as he and Samantha came home that evening. His daughter echoed the sentiment.

'I've missed you, too,' Helen said lightly, her glance embracing them both. She looked away quickly before answering the question he asked her, unable to meet his eyes as she assured him that she was feeling fine now, that her headache had disappeared hours ago.

Her headache had disappeared—but she was feeling far from fine. On seeing him she had suffered an inexplicable attack of nervousness. It was so bad that her hands had started to tremble, and she held them firmly together in her lap as Scot came over to her.

'I'm glad to hear it, because I'm taking you out to dinner tonight.'

'Dinner?' she queried.

'Not that that's anything to get excited about,' he grinned. 'The entertainment scene here is far from sophisticated, so don't bother putting on your gold lamé!'

She gave him a half-hearted smile. 'I haven't brought it with me.' She was fazed, wondering what she should wear, wondering why she felt suddenly tongue-tied, why suddenly she wished she had not found out who Scot really was, why she was considering not tackling him about it at all.

And her nervousness increased by the minute. The

sadness was still there, too. She felt that everything had been spoiled, she was disillusioned, feeling that Scot had deceived her.

But that didn't stop her from taking care with her make-up, from picking out a suitable dress to wear. It was a simple summer dress in blue, the same shade as her eyes, edged with broderie anglaise around the hemline and neckline.

Nor did it stop her from loving him. She closed her eyes and swallowed against the lump in her throat. What good was it? What use was there in loving him? He would never ask to see her again when they parted company next week. Although he had not asked for her address, she had nevertheless nursed the hope that he might, telling herself that there was time yet, several days of it. Now, however, she knew for certain that he would not want to see her again. They were, they really were just ships that passed in the night, after all.

And they came from different worlds.

Over dinner, when they were halfway through their main course of local Bahamian fish, Scot asked her what was wrong.

Helen wasn't tasting what she was eating. She had tried all sorts of fish while staying here, the delicately flavoured snapper, the more tasty grouper, and the large shellfish, conch, which was the staple diet of the locals. By Lizzy she had been given Bahamian peas and rice, conch fritters and chowder, and she had eaten avocados, which were expensive at home, to her heart's content. Yes, she had really enjoyed the food in the West Indies.

Tonight, however, the lobster she was eating tasted like old newspaper. Even the wine didn't help, though both the wine and the food were, she felt sure, excellent. Scot was obviously enjoying both . . .

'Helen, what's wrong? Are you sure you're feeling okay?'

She put a smile on her face. 'I'm fine, Scot!'

He grimaced. 'A plastic smile, if ever I saw one. You've been giving me one-word answers all evening and you haven't volunteered an ounce of conversation. So, what did you do with yourself today?'

This was her opportunity, the perfect cue. She looked straight into his eyes—and her courage failed her. What was wrong with her? Why couldn't she broach the subject? Why was she feeling as nervous as she had on her very first date years ago? 'Oh, nothing much,' she managed. 'I read a lot.'

Scot took over. He kept a conversation going, coaxing her to contribute, and she marvelled yet again at his ability to bring her out. But she was far from being wholly herself tonight, as she had been with him hitherto.

When he suggested that they move on to the night club after dinner, Helen jumped at the chance.

'Well, a little enthusiasm at last! I hope you're not disappointed.' He took hold of her hand and linked it through his arm as they left the hotel restaurant.

Helen tried very hard to relax, but she couldn't. Scot's arm was supporting hers in a gentlemanly, old-fashioned way, a gesture that she liked, but the feel of him, the physical contact with him made her all the more jumpy. All she could think of then was that she loved this man, she wanted him, but there was no light at the end of this particular tunnel, no hope of anything more than a holiday romance.

As they were seated in the night club, she could hear Scot's voice in her head, telling her angrily that he had had more women that he cared to remember. She could bet her life on *that*!

She looked at him almost furtively, not realising that suspicion was showing in her eyes. Had he been a road sweeper he would still be attractive to women. He was a striking, handsome man with the kind of physique which would make any woman look twice. But he wasn't a road sweeper, he was famous. He was talented and suave and sophisticated, and women probably fell at his feet.

He wasn't turning any heads tonight, however, but that was only because the lights in this place were so dim. The club was fairly rough and ready, actually, with white walls of rough-cast plaster, draped with the occasional fishing net and stuffed fish by way of decoration. On the candlelit tables was a list of the house's speciality cocktails—Bahama Mama, Goombay Smash, Piña Coloda and a myriad selection of rum punches which were decorated with fruit.

Still, the place had atmosphere. There were five people on a tiny stage playing calypso music which Helen would have enjoyed very much at any other time.

'You're mad at me, aren't you?' Scot said at one point.

'I—about what?' Helen looked at him warily. Had he guessed that she knew who he was?

'Last night.'

'Last night?' She had no idea what he was talking about until she remembered the pass he had made, a no-nonsense and very serious pass, and with the memory came a certain embarrassment which she had never thought to feel with Scot. But oh, how easy it would have been—how easy it would be—to join the ranks of women in his casual affairs. Helen stiffened at the idea. No way. There was no way she would let that happen!

Scot saw her reaction and said, 'I thought so. Look, Helen——'

'No, actually I'm not cross about that. You told me I shouldn't blame a man for trying, didn't you?'

'Then don't,' he grinned. 'And stop thinking I have lascivious and dishonourable ulterior motives for giving you this wild and decadent night out.' The grin developed into that incredibly attractive smile. 'I'll say one thing for me—I know when to take no for an answer!'

He bent his head towards her, his eyes twinkling as he continued to tease her and coax a response from her. 'But you are going to dance with me now, mm?'

Helen felt tears prickling at the back of her eyes. 'Scot, may I have something else to drink? I find this cocktail a bit sickly.'

'Sick——? All right,' he said softly, 'that does it. Come on, let's get out of here.'

He wasn't cross, she realised as they drove back to the villa, he was resigned. She steeled herself as he brought the car to a halt at the back of the house. 'Scot, I—let's stay up for a nightcap. I want to talk to you.'

She had rehearsed in the car what she would say to him, knowing she couldn't go on like this, creating this atmosphere. While Lizzy was saying goodnight and reporting on Sam, Helen went over her opening speech again. But it didn't come out right.

Scot mixed drinks for them. He handed her a gin and tonic and sat facing her, looking at her expectantly—which made matters worse.

'I found—there are some cassettes in that cupboard over there . . .'

'Yes,' he said patiently, obviously at a loss. 'And a few hundred records, too—Corinne's a music buff. So?'

'Some unmarked cassettes. I mean, tapes with no printed labels on them.'

When he still looked blank she went on, 'I don't know whether they actually belong to Corinne or whether they're yours. It doesn't matter. What matters is that——' Helen stopped abruptly, her uncertainty changing rapidly into annoyance. Why the hell was she beating about the bush when it was he who had deceived her? 'Put it this way,' she said stiffly, 'do you think I know you well enough now to start calling you "Maestro"?'

She saw his eyebrows go up, she watched his hairline move back as surprise spread over his features. She saw, and almost took pleasure in, the look of disappointment which followed his initial reaction. 'I've been rumbled,' he said dully.

'Yes, Mr Montague, you've been rumbled. Or sussed out, as we might put it in England.'

He searched the blueness of her eyes, a grim expression on his face. 'And?'

'And why the hell didn't you tell me? Why couldn't you have trusted me with this information? What did you think I would do—tip off the dreaded reporters as to where your secret hideout is? Honestly!'

'No, Helen, I never thought that for a moment.'

She sighed, feeling more upset than anything else. 'I understand much more now, Scot. I understand why Lizzy never let me know who you are, I understand your need to have at least one private place in the world. What I don't understand is why you never had the faith in me, the trust in me, to tell me.'

'Trust? Helen, I trust you implicitly, you should know that by now.' He sighed heavily, dragging his fingers through his thick fair hair. 'Helen, you don't understand.'

'No, I——'

'Please! Please, please don't be mad. I can see you're disappointed, but don't be mad. I can explain it all. It's just—it'll take a while. Bear with me.'

Helen sank back against the cushions. She wasn't angry, not any longer. There was something about his attitude, a look of sudden tiredness about him, which put her immediately on his side. Loving him helped too, of course; loving him made her want to listen. Quietly she said, 'It's funny, isn't it? I said you don't look like a pianist. Of course you're much more than that, but it's on the piano that you do your creating, and now ...' She laughed a little, shaking her head. 'And now I can't imagine you being or doing anything else.'

Scot stared at her, his eyes narrowing as he did so. Then he nodded briefly, once, as if what she had just said made perfect sense to him. 'Helen, if you'll think about what you've just said, you'll begin to understand why I didn't tell you my professional name, that day you asked me about my work. It's for precisely that reason that I didn't tell you. My real name *is* Marcus Scot—it was changed for professional reasons—and it's Marcus Scot I wanted you to know and like. I didn't want you to associate me with something—anything in particular. I didn't want you to think of me as Scot Montague the composer or the lyricist or whatever. I wanted you to think of me as Marcus Scot, the *man*.

That's what I wanted, for you to have no preconceived ideas, no prejudices good or bad. Surely this makes sense to you?'

She didn't hesitate. 'Yes. Yes, it makes perfect sense. But I'm not the sort of person who's awestruck by meeting someone famous. I have tremendous respect for your talent, for all that you do and have done, but I certainly don't think of you as superhuman or something. You *could* have told me.'

Scot didn't say anything for a moment. He got up and switched on a couple of lamps, turning off the overhead light. Then he went to the bar and topped up his drink.

'That isn't true,' he said at length. 'Hell, this might sound horribly conceited to you, but there are very few people, very few people, who treat me merely as a person. A person in my own right. Corinne does, of course, but she's known me for years. She knew me before I was—a name. In fact it was she who helped me to make that name.

'What I'm trying to say is that if you had known earlier who I am, our relationship might not have developed the way it has. You'll deny that, I know, but it's true. This is very difficult to explain, but an—an odd sort of change occurs in people, the non-famous, when they find themselves in the company of the famous. It's probably because when a person is very well known, his or her reputation tends to precede them wherever they go or whatever they do. It happened to me in my early days in show business, when I met the big names, people I'd regarded in my youth as some kind of heroes, people I'd admired. Does this make sense to you, Helen? Do you see what I mean?'

'Perfectly.' She meant it, too. 'I understand, I understand. But you're forgetting that I'm not American. You've had no publicity as such in England, so there was no reputation to precede you, to colour my judgment of you as a person—one way or another.'

'But look at you now,' he pointed out. 'Look at this evening. You've been stiff and stilted and unnatural with me all evening, and you can't tell me it has nothing to do with my being Scot Montague. Already it's created a change in you. You're not yourself, and that saddens me, Helen. It saddens me because I like you enormously, because you're the first *real* person I've met in a very long time.'

'Just a moment . . .' Helen paused, realising that her answer needed a little thought. She had understood all he had explained and, she had to admit, to a large extent he was right. In the last three weeks she had discovered so much about the man. She had known nothing about the name. Had she known who he was, she might have treated each and every discovery with something like, 'Fancy Scot Montague being . . . this or that.'

She looked at him evenly, inclining her head as she conceded the point. 'You're right, Scot. You wouldn't have started out with me as an unmarked—as a blackboard on which nothing had been written, if I may put it like that. But . . . but I still feel let down.'

'Let down?' he queried.

'Yes. I mean—would you have told me, some time?'

'Of course!'

Cautiously, not wishing to lack subtlety, she asked, 'Why would you have bothered to tell me? Why not let me go home thinking merely that I'd met a nice man while I was on holiday?'

'Ah, Helen . . .' his smile was sad, 'I hope that's how you'll think of me, regardless. That would be very precious to me. You see, my darling, what I feel for you goes further than mere liking.'

His clear green eyes held hers and Helen's heart accelerated wildly, its rhythm thrumming somewhere in the base of her throat.

'To answer your question,' he went on, 'I was intending to tell you, very soon, who I am. For two good reasons. Firstly there's every chance that I'll be collared by people, reporters or members of the public, when we're together in America. And I didn't want you to find out that way. And secondly, I want very much to see you again. In the future, if you're willing . . .'

This time, her heart jumped crazily in her breast and she was grateful that he was crossing the room, sitting down again, and couldn't see her face.

'How long are you going to hesitate, Helen?' he asked quietly as his eyes met hers. He cursed softly, almost inaudibly. 'Dammit, you are disappointed, aren't you? I can't decide what's spoiling things between us—the fact that I didn't tell you myself or the fact that I *am* Scot Montague.'

'Neither,' she said, when she could trust herself to speak with a steady voice. 'You've explained your reasons for withholding, and as for your being Scot Montague—well, that doesn't matter one way or another to me. I'm impressed, but I'm not about to pester you for your autograph, if that's what you're worried about!'

'And what about Marcus? Were you impressed with him?'

Her eyes closed briefly and she nodded. She had to answer that one honestly, it mattered a great deal to him. 'Very much so.'

Something approaching relief flicked across his face. 'So far so good.' A ghost of a smile touched his lips. 'You never gave me your answer—about our meeting again in England.'

'The answer is yes.' She said it without hesitating, but she also said it with just a slight touch of nonchalance. Somewhere in the back of her mind she was wishing she'd had the strength to say no. After all, what was the point? A girl such as she, a man such as he—the two just didn't add up. 'What did you say, Scot?'

'I said I'll make a deal with you.' He was rifling through a drawer in a pine wood bureau against the wall. When he found what he was looking for—a pad and a pen—he handed them to her. 'Write your telephone number and your address on there. Tear off the page and give it to me.'

Helen did as he asked, wondering what the deal was.

'Right.' Scott took the paper from her, folded it without even glancing at it, and put it in his jacket pocket. 'Here's the deal. By the time I've finished talking to you tonight, if you want the piece of paper back, you can have it back. I haven't even looked at it. Okay?'

She frowned, bemused. 'Okay. Are you going to explain yourself—I hope!'

He didn't smile. 'I'm going to tell you about Scot Montague,' he said wryly. 'He's overshadowed Marcus for a very long time, but if you really were impressed with Marcus then I needn't worry too much about what Scot Montague might do to you. In other words, Helen, if our foundation is strong enough, you'll tell me to keep that piece of paper.'

Helen's eyes widened in surprise. 'Scot, you don't have to——.'

'But I do—I certainly do.'

She expelled a long, nervous breath, her eyes trailing after him as he went to the bar and refilled their glasses.

'I told you that Samantha had been injured in a road accident,' he began. 'And where was Scot Montague when it happened? Where was the child's father? Getting steadily bombed in the apartment of some would-be starlet I'd picked up for a one-night stand.'

Helen bit hard on her lip and said nothing. She would let him talk. She would make no comment until she'd heard it all. Oh, but the bitterness in his voice when next he spoke, the self-disgust made her heart twist painfully.

'Sam almost died. Her skull was fractured, her injuries were extensive and she was unconscious for almost a day. When she came to, they still hadn't located me. Nobody knew where the hell I was! I hardly knew myself. I was living it up, indulging, in every sense of the word, with a girl who was a stranger to me. How do you like that?'

Helen closed her eyes against the expression on his face. He didn't expect an answer.

'Everyone had been looking for me for hours, the

police included. Samantha came to and found Bessie by her bed, my housekeeper. My housekeeper and Corrie. And one or two of my .. : retinue ... were hovering outside in the hospital corridor. A lovely state of affairs—everyone but her father! He was busy——'

'Scot, Scot ...' Helen couldn't help herself, his fury was frightening '... where was Sam's mother?'

'Her *what*?' He got to his feet, looking at Helen as though she'd said something filthy. 'Doing something similar to what I was doing, I've no doubt. Oh, she sent a get well card two days later, when the news of Sam's accident was plastered all over the newspapers. And do you know how this item of news was presented to the public? With a photograph of me dashing in to the hospital, when I was finally told of the news. This, thanks to Corinne. She had somehow managed to keep the news of the accident of Scot Montague's daughter under wraps for a day—God knows how! It'll have cost her a few dollars, make no mistake.'

He shrugged, pacing about like a frustrated animal. 'So I was presented nicely as the concerned father. What hypocrisy, what sheer, bloody hypocrisy! When I came to my senses, I wanted to tell the press what had really happened. That I hadn't *cared* about my own little girl for a long time, never mind that one lost day.'

'That can't be true, Scot. It can't be! I can see you love her!'

He sat down heavily, his voice level but solemn now, without emotion of any kind. 'No. Actually, it isn't true. Let's just say I ... I'd forgotten how to show that I care.'

He looked up suddenly, going off at a tangent which Helen was grateful for later on. It helped to present the picture as a whole. 'I was born in Sussex. When I was eleven, my parents emigrated. They were both doctors. I have one brother who's four years older than I and who's also a doctor, living in England now. I too went to medical school in the States, following my brother's footsteps, following my parents' footsteps. Of course, it didn't work. My talents lay in a very different direction and my parents had known this all along, as I obviously had. I was—trying to please my old man, I suppose, as you were with your father when you went to university.

'Anyhow, to cut a long story short I moved to New York City from the comfort of a middle-class home in Cleveland, Ohio, to a rented attic in Manhattan, where it was all happening. I met Corinne, a rich lady with a film producer for a husband, and she had all the contacts I needed to set me on the path to—wherever it is I've ended up. And that's open to question,' he added with a self-deprecating smile.

'Corinne has worked as both agent and manager for me. She's a great girl and a good friend. It was she who introduced me to my wife, but I'll forgive her for that single error. I was living in Los Angeles by the time I met her—Hannah Douglas, as she calls herself now. She was Hannah Fowls when I met her.'

Hannah Douglas. It was another name very familiar to Helen. But in this case, so was the face, a very beautiful face. Hannah Douglas was a film actress.

'I hadn't made it in a big way at that point, but I was on the road to success—and Hannah knew it, too. She was my only girl-friend at the time—my wilder days came later—and her proposal to me was an unusual one, to say the least. She told me one day, "I'm expecting your baby, Scot. What do you want to do about it? Shall I get rid of it, or shall we get married?" We got married.'

He leaned back, lit a cigarette and glanced in the direction of the upstairs bedrooms. 'At least one good thing came out of the marriage. But you know, Helen, I was still quite wet behind the ears in those days. I never realised how ambitious Hannah was until the day when she threw Samantha at me and, God help me, I mean that literally. The baby was seven or eight months old, and it wasn't until later that I realised Hannah must have been on the point of murdering the child. And it wasn't as if she had to look after the baby twenty-fours hours a day—far from it. But her frustrations went beyond the fact that she felt saddled with Sam and a marriage she no longer wanted.'

Scot was looking beyond Helen now, unseeing, a muscle jerking in his jaw as he remembered. 'It was a bad scene. In deference to you, I'll keep it clean and give you the essence of the things she screamed at me that day. 'I'm sick of playing mother to your brat. I'm sick of being Scot Montague's wife, I'm sick of playing second fiddle to the sort of career I can get for myself—*for myself*!'

There was silence.

'Since you're telling me all this,' Helen said at length, 'then be wholly honest. Your marriage was—what? Six months old?'

'Something like that.'

'And were you unfaithful to Hannah? Did she find out?'

His laughter was hollow. 'I was faithful every day and night of my marriage. I'm not quite the wolf you imagine me to be, Helen, though I can't blame you for imagining. Most of the time it's been—I don't know, an escape of some sort. Crazy though that might sound.' He shrugged. 'The women are there, always, and in the kind of circles I mix in they're mostly——'

'Beautiful.'

'"Easy" was the word I was going to use. A lot of them are hangers-on or ambitious for themselves.' He smiled at her, and this time his smile was genuine because it reached and softened his eyes. Because it was for her, about her. 'But I've already told you, you're the first real woman I've met in a long time.'

She wasn't, nor had she been earlier, sure what Scot meant by this. But now was not the time to question him about it. 'I take it Hannah walked out?'

'Sure. She had what she wanted by then, you see. She'd learned a lot, she had the contacts she needed to pursue her own career. And she put them to good use,' he added cynically. 'In her own particular fashion. She's not a particularly talented actress. She's just famous and beautiful to look at.'

Helen looked down at the floor as the implication

sank in. 'And you? How did you take all this? What happened to you?'

'With a certain amount of relief, I have to confess. It was all wrong from the day we signed the register, we both knew that really. What happened to me? I got more and more successful. Three years ago I made it in a very big way.'

'With the "Lady Love" theme.'

'Yes.'

'And a couple of months ago you won an Oscar. You're still riding high, Scot. You're at the zenith of your career now.'

'I'm finished,' he corrected. 'When I've met the commitments I have in hand, fulfilled my contracts, I'm finished.'

'But——'

'By choice. I'm getting out of that scene, out of that life. America's a great country, but it's got to the stage now where I'm recognised on the street. The success of "Lady Love" brought me a great deal of publicity, television chat shows, interviews for magazines, the papers and so on—and Corinne's milked every drop she could from these opportunities.'

'Surely she was only doing her job?'

'Of course. Don't misunderstand me, Helen. I loved it at the time.' He broke off, searching her eyes for understanding. 'But, while over the years I got more and more successful as an artist, I managed in the process to lose my*self*, my own identity. I hated the person I had become, but it took Sam's accident to make me realise what I'd become. I'd been riding the crest of a wave, living in the kind of society where nothing matters except success. I was caught up in the glitter of it all, the publicity, the parties, the kudos . . .'

Helen was pensive as she tried to imagine the kind of life he had been leading, a lifestyle which was so alien to her. 'And Sam's accident brought you crashing back down to earth?'

Scot flinched at the memory. It gave Helen just an inkling of what he must have been through when he nearly lost his daughter. 'It almost destroyed me. The reformation began right then. It started with the kind of pain I can't describe to you, the self-loathing, the realisation that I'd lost touch with the things that really matter in this life. I didn't even realise how precious Sam is to me until I almost lost her.

'There was one week, the third week she was in hospital, when I drank myself into a stupor. But that's something I don't regret because, strange though it sounds, I emerged from it with a sharpness and clarity of mind and purpose which will never leave me now. I'd been through hell. But it was as if—as if I had to go through it in order to—what can I say? To be given a second chance.

'When I learned that I'd been nominated for an Academy award, I was unmoved. I didn't attend the function—someone else received it on my behalf. Since then I've been hounded for interviews with all sorts of media—which I've refused in no uncertain terms.'

Silence reigned.

At length he said, 'I think that brings us up to date. Except to say I thank God children are so resilient. Do you know what Sam said to me, one day in the hospital? 'I'm glad we're going to be together more now, Scot. We can be friends, can't we?'

He looked sadly at Helen. 'It's only recently that she's started to call me Daddy. "Friends" . . . as if that were some sort of treat! And all she asked of me was that I take her to Disneyland when she was better. I did that, when the doctor gave me the okay. But Samantha wasn't as well as she appeared to be. She was still getting the occasional headache and we'd only been there a couple of hours when the excitement brought one on. And I'd been tailed there by some reporter guy who had his notebook and camera at the ready. I don't know how I stopped myself from punching him when he approached us.'

'So then you came here, and you thought I was someone else who'd followed you. I'm glad you didn't punch me.'

It didn't work. She had hoped to bring a smile to his face, but she failed. He was looking at her intently, waiting for her to say something constructive. In fact he was, she felt, waiting for her to pass judgment. 'So you've got to know your daughter. She's had a good rest here. She's fully recovered now and holding you to your promise about Disneyland–World.'

That brought a smile. A humourless smile. 'I want to know,' Scot said quietly, firmly, 'I want to know what you want me to do with that piece of paper you gave me.'

Helen didn't stop to think about what she was doing, she was concerned only with reassuring him. She went over to him and sat on the arm of his chair and ran her fingers through the thickness of his hair. 'Keep it. Keep it, Scot, and listen to me now. I can't say whether it was right of you or wrong of you to have lived the way you have. To a certain extent, I'm sure you had no choice. I'm sure the high life, the glitter, the publicity and the parties are inevitable in a career such as yours. At least, they would be very hard to avoid when your object was to be a success; it's only natural that the public would want to know about you. Your songs have given a great deal of pleasure to millions of people.'

She smiled, turning his head so that she could look him straight in the eyes. 'You're not such a bad guy. All right, so you made a few mistakes in the domestic side of your life. But nobody's proud of a marriage that fails, and this probably affected you more than you realise. You spoke of your subsequent affairs as being some sort of escape——'

'They weren't affairs. They didn't last long enough to merit that description.'

'Which goes part way to proving what I was about to say——'

He put a finger over her lips. 'Let me say it. That way you'll see that I've learned a thing or two. I used to drink heavily, but I've cut down drastically since I came to my senses. That was a form of escape, too. You see, despite everything I've achieved, I can't describe myself as being happy over the past three or four years. Perhaps at some subconscious level I knew I was turning into someone else—someone I didn't like. But you can't escape by drinking any more than you can escape in the arms of a woman who represents nothing more than sexual gratification—or a woman who's using you, eager to go to bed with you for what she might get out of it, a means of advancing her own career, perhaps, or the questionable kick of being able to tell her friends she's slept with Scot Montague.'

Helen drew away from him, stepping back so she could look at him. She put her hands on her hips and shook her head. 'Stop it! Don't be bitter with yourself, Scot. Let go of the past. It's history, and remember what you told me.' Gently, she added, 'That there's nothing anyone can do, ever, to change what has happened in the past. It's the quality of your future life that's important now.'

CHAPTER EIGHT

DISNEY World really was a world on its own. It not only lived up to Helen's expectations, it surpassed them. She found herself talking to Mickey Mouse and having her photograph taken with a life-size Yogi Bear.

She and Scot and a delighted Samantha explored the Magic Kingdom, the Haunted House, Fantasyland and Tomorrowland. They sailed, they walked, they rode the old railroad and the modern monorail which skirted the enormous park. They saw banjo-playing bears which were so life-like, so brilliantly operated that one almost forgot they weren't real. They saw cowboys and Indians, pirates, famous historical figures, animals, arcades, shops, shows, water-skiing displays, dances— and a great many fascinated and carefree sightseers, old as well as young.

Helen was exhausted after the second day, exhausted but looking forward to the next day, Wednesday, which would be their last at Disney World. She would be flying back to England on Thursday night, not because she wanted to but because she had to. With an eight-hour journey to London, and bearing in mind the time difference between her own country and Florida, she had booked the Thursday night flight in order to give herself a chance to recover before she went in to work. It was the only sensible thing to do.

It was hot in Florida. After her weeks in the West Indies she could cope with day-long sunshine well enough, but the humidity here did not exactly help her to cope with all her activity! After two days at Disney World, they had by no means seen all there was to see, done all there was to do. Helen said as much to Scot when they all got into the car at the end of the second day.

'Well, we'll just have to see all we can tomorrow,' he said.

'You!' Helen giggled. 'You're not as bored as you expected to be, are you?'

He grinned at her as he manoeuvred the car easily out of the vast car park. 'Okay, I'll come clean! I'm enjoying myself ... but that isn't wholly because I've got Disney World to look at.'

Helen smiled at the compliment, relaxing as the air-conditioning came on in the car. Scot had organised everything very well indeed. After sailing from the Bahamas they had flown in a privately hired plane to Orlando. At Orlando there had been a car waiting for them, the one they were in. It was on hire, an American car, long and sleek and comfortable, but Scot had referred to it as an ordinary family saloon which was not likely to attract any attention.

He had been recognised several times, in fact. Helen had seen a few people nudging one another and nodding in Scot's direction, but only two people had actually came up to him and asked for his autograph, which he had given with a smile, without fuss or any sign of irritation. He had not been accosted by anyone from the media, however, for which Helen was grateful.

They were staying at an inn a few miles from Lake Poinsett. It was a fairly small, family-run place which served good food, was comfortable if not luxurious, and its owners had been only too willing to keep check on the sleeping Samantha the previous evening while Scot took Helen out to dinner.

Scot said that the people who owned the inn were friends of a friend of a friend, but he had nevertheless signed the register as Marcus Scot. Of course the owners knew full well who he was, but they weren't going to broadcast it to their other guests.

'The price of fame,' Helen had remarked after they'd been shown to their rooms on their arrival.

'A high price—too high,' Scot had replied. 'I'm sorry, Helen, I realise this may all seem a little neurotic to you. And I'm sorry that this place can't be described as anything other than homely, but I don't want to be hassled. I want you all to myself.'

Helen didn't mind in the least. The feeling was mutual.

Samantha was sound asleep on the back seat of the car now, exhausted after her busy day. She looked like an angel with her blonde curls framing her face—such a pretty face. Looking at her, Helen felt a sudden stab of jealousy which she hated herself for. Not only was it out of character, it was pointless—as jealousy always is. She had looked at Samantha and thought of her as the product of the union of Hannah Douglas and Scot Montague. Hannah Fowls and Marcus Scot. And with that thought came the stab of jealousy.

She looked at Scot, loving him, as he gathered his daughter into his arms and carried her indoors. If Helen were to have a child, his child, what would she be like? Or what would he be like? Would Scot like to have another child? Would he like a son?

'Do you want to eat in or eat out tonight, my darling?' Scot's voice broke in to her thoughts. He'd started to use the endearment often and it was always, always preceded by the possessive.

'In. I'm too tired to make the effort to go out. I just want to have forty winks and then shower and put on something very comfortable.'

'Sounds good to me!' He gave her a roguish grin. 'You do just that—slip into something comfortable and come up and see me some time!'

Helen had only to go next door but one to see him, to the other side of Sam's room. She slept for a while and then she showered and washed and dried her hair, which she gathered into a ponytail before pulling on a pair of jeans and a pale lemon blouse.

Scot teased her mercilessly as he opened the door to her. Samantha was in his room, having been fed earlier with the young children of other guests, and he kept Helen at the door for a moment so that Sam was out of earshot. 'That isn't the sexiest outfit I've seen you wearing. You can do better than that!'

Helen leaned against the door jamb, folding her arms

in an attitude of boredom. 'I'll say this for you, you get ten out of ten for trying!'

They had exchanged a lot of this type of banter. She was well aware that Scot was intrigued by her refusal to go to bed with him. She was different. She was different and she was real—and she had soon come to realise what he had meant by that, when she had given thought to all he had told her about his recent years and the people who moved in his orbit.

What he didn't know was that she was actually on guard constantly, tinglingly aware of his sexuality, his virile masculinity, during every waking minute, no matter what they were doing. It would be all too easy to succumb to the powerful physical attraction she felt towards him. But where would that leave her? As just another statistic. And it would be bad enough parting from him as it was, without having known the fullest extent of his lovemaking.

'Miss Good, you're a hard woman. I suspect you're frigid. Or is it just that you insist on living up to your name?'

Helen faked a yawn. 'Can you imagine how many other people have made remarks like that to me?'

He pushed the door open. 'So I lack originality! Come in.'

The telephone rang, and Helen's eyebrows went up in surprise.

'I've been trying to get through to Corinne at the Dorchester,' Scot explained hastily. 'It's high time I let her know where I am. That's probably the operator now.' He picked up the telephone and sat down. 'Yes, I booked the call person-to-person.' He put his hand over the mouthpiece while he was waiting. 'Hey, Sam, move off that chair and let Helen sit down.'

There were only two armchairs in the room and Scot was using one of them. Sam vacated hers and climbed on to Helen's lap as she sat, whispering, 'Helen, you're sitting on Jemima's leg!'

Helen freed Jemima from her discomfort and looked uncertainly at Scot, wondering whether he might prefer privacy while he spoke to his agent. 'Would you rather—I mean, shall I come back in ten minutes or so?'

'Of course not! You just relax, my darling ... Corrie? Hi, it's me.'

Helen obviously couldn't help hearing all that followed. Scot's side of the conversation, at least. She was close enough to hear the sound of Corinne's voice from time to time, though she couldn't make out what she said.

After a brief pause Scot said, 'Florida—yes, that's what I said, Florida. Well, that's a long story. I found it impossible to stay in Beverly Hills—my address is hardly a secret, Corinne. ... Yes, they were hovering like hawks. It was hardly better even in Disneyland. Yes, we went there, but Samantha had a slight relapse ... Sure, she's fine now, fighting fit. Anyhow, we went to Trinini. I thought——'

He was interrupted by an excited babble from Corinne, which he calmly put a stop to. 'I know. Relax, will you? I know that isn't what I told you, but I had to change my plans. I had to escape in order to concentrate on Sam—and can you think of anywhere better?'

There was a sudden exclamation from Corinne, and Helen smiled. Corinne had just realised that the villa had already been occupied!

Scot was laughing. 'Helen? Yes, I ran into her. I certainly did! ... Fine, fine. We stayed on together ... You're not half as surprised as I was, believe me! As a matter of fact, she's here with me right now ...'

There was another exclamation. Scot said a few words about Disney World and the inn where they were staying—and Helen found herself wishing she could hear what Corinne had to say about all this, because Scot was now saying, 'She is—I couldn't agree with you more. I'll do that.'

After a moment or two, the laughter faded from his eyes. His expression tightened and he reached for a pack of cigarettes. 'Of course you're right,' he said gruffly. 'I know it. Believe me, I'm well aware of it. I'll

have to work day and night to make up for lost time . . .
Corinne, will you *cool* it?'

Helen began to feel ill at ease. She was cuddling
Samantha, who in turn was cuddling her doll. Scot was
clearly talking business now, and she felt she ought to
leave the room. 'Come on, sweetheart,' she said to Sam.
'I'll put you to bed, and Daddy will come in and see
you when he's finished his phone call.'

She signalled Scot as to her intentions and he put his
hand over the mouthpiece. 'All right, thanks. I'll see
you in the bar downstairs.'

There was a small bar in the inn, adjoining the dining
room, and Helen had been there for ten minutes before
Scot arrived. She had ordered a drink for him and was
pleased to see him smiling when he joined her.

'Corinne was full of compliments about you,' he
announced. 'She said you were a sweet and sensitive
girl, and I told her I couldn't agree more.' He raised his
glass in a toast to Helen, his green eyes smiling at her
warmly. 'And she sent you her love.'

Helen was touched, very much so. 'How nice! Thank
you. I take it she's all right?'

'Mad as hell because I haven't contacted her all this
time. She told me she'd been killing time, waiting to
hear from me. Of course she had no idea I'd gone to the
villa. I said, "Since when do you call shopping a means
of killing time?" '

'And she said?'

'Something very unladylike,' Scot grinned. 'Then she
reminded me that she'd been working on my behalf, not
having fun.'

Helen laughed. This had obviously taken place after
she had left Scot's room, and she couldn't imagine
Corinne saying something very unladylike.

'She said she'll fly back to Los Angeles tomorrow,
now she's heard from me,' he went on. 'I told her I'd be
home soon.'

His words affected Helen badly. How short it was
now, their time together. 'I take it she's found you a
house?'

He sighed. 'No, she's had no luck. I'm a bit surprised, because she's put one hundred per cent effort into it, and I thought that she, of all people, would come up with results.'

'I'm surprised, too,' Helen admitted. 'I mean, it's still very much a buyer's market in England. In any case, I should think—er—well, I suppose money presents no problem to you?'

Scot smiled as though she had said something incredibly naïve. 'None at all. It isn't that, it's the stipulations I've laid down which made things a little more difficult, I suppose.'

'Stipulations?'

He shrugged. 'I don't want a modern house, I want something fairly old, something with character about it. It has to be reasonably near the capital but out in the country, off the beaten track. I want a decent amount of land surrounding it. I intend to keep a couple of horses, to have an extension which will house a swimming pool, if there isn't one there already, and enough room so that I can have a soundproofed studio built in. I won't be in any hurry for that, but I'll want it eventually. And of course there must be room for an apartment for my housekeeper. Bessie's coming with me.'

'Well! You're looking for—for an estate, Scot! Houses like that don't come on to the market every day.'

'Quite. Corinne looked at a few places, which she rejected. She'll be keeping in touch from L.A. with several of the real estate agents she's been dealing with. Something will come up, given time.'

'I . . . see.' It was very difficult for Helen to hide her disappointment, she had to force herself to be casual. 'So you've no idea when you'll be coming to England? I assume this brief visit you spoke of was in order that you could inspect your would-be home? You—said you'd be going to England for one or two nights.'

'That's right. Corinne will deal with everything. All that will remain for me to do is look at the house she picks out and say yes or no. Yes, I hope. As for when this will happen—your guess is as good as mine.'

There was a sudden silence. They were sitting in the corner of the room and none of the other occupants of the bar were paying any attention to them. For all the world they appeared to be two ordinary people having a pre-dinner drink in the bar of an ordinary inn. But that wasn't the case. Scot was not an ordinary, average person, and never before had Helen felt this as strongly as she felt it now.

She wished they didn't come from such vastly different backgrounds. She wished she didn't love him. She wished she didn't feel so wretchedly disappointed at not knowing when she would see him again. *If* she would see him again . . .

She cleared her throat. 'Corinne—Corinne really is a good friend, isn't she? I—mean all this isn't part of her role as agent and manager.'

If Scot was aware of any change in Helen's attitude, of the intrusion of a sudden awkwardness between them, he didn't show it. 'I don't know what I'd do without her. She's a great girl.' He finished what was left of his drink and took hold of Helen's hand. 'Are you ready to eat now, my darling?'

She brightened at once. The look in his eyes, the endearment and the firm, warm grip of his hand holding hers was the reassurance she desperately needed. 'Ready?' She was almost indignant. 'I'm positively famished!'

Scot laughed softly, shaking his head as he steered her towards the dining room. 'Ah, Helen! Helen, Helen, Helen, you're such a breath of fresh air! Some of the sayings you come out with, they're familiar to me and yet strange on my ears. You're so *English* at times!'

They said goodbye to Disney World at three the following afternoon. The level of humidity in Florida seemed to be increasing by the day, and while Helen was loath to waste precious time by taking an afternoon nap, she knew she would have to. Scot was taking her out to dinner tonight and for this, their last night, she wanted to be fresh, to look her best.

All day it had hung over them—not just Helen but over Scot and Samantha, too—that this was their last day of their vacation, their last full day together. Tomorrow they would be flying back to Miami, to the airport. Scot had organised his flight from there, picking his time as close to Helen's departure as he could.

She dressed on that Wednesday evening with a great deal of care, taking pains with her make-up and brushing her silky, jet-black hair until it shone. She had brought with her a white dress which she had not yet worn. It was hand-crocheted in fine cotton, a pretty, lacy dress for which she had paid a lot of money almost a year ago in a London boutique. And she had never worn it at all. In fact, had she been thinking properly at the time she had packed for this holiday, she would not have put it in her suitcase, she would have considered it unsuitable for the sort of holiday she had planned on taking ... away from civilisation.

Scot's eyes told her of his approval as soon as she opened her door to him. He looked at her appreciatively, his clear green eyes moving downwards and then slowly upwards before coming to rest on her face. 'You look beautiful, Helen. You *are* beautiful.'

She inclined her head, her attitude nothing short of flirtatious, inviting. 'Why, thank you, kind sir.' She took his arm as they went out to the car.

If Helen looked beautiful, Scot was striking in his handsomeness. He was wearing blue slacks which were immaculately cut, a matching shirt and a lightweight, navy blue jacket and navy tie. She had never seen him looking quite this smart, though his thick blond mane was as unruly as ever, curling slightly at the collar and falling on to his forehead at will.

Helen reached up and raked her fingers through it, the way he so often did. 'Where are we dining?' They were in the car park and Scot was fishing in his pocket for the car keys.

Her gesture with his hair seemed to please him. He forgot his quest for the keys and caught hold of her around the waist, looking down at her with a strange and unreadable expression in his eyes. 'Helen, I . . .' He got no further. He shook his head briefly, communicating to her by doing so that he thought this neither the time nor the place to say what he'd been about to say.

They dined in the Cocoa Beach area. They had a corner table in an expensive, open-air restaurant which was fringed with palm trees. The soft strains of romantic music drifted over from the adjoining, covered dining area and from only a few yards away there was the sound of the sea swishing gently against the sands.

Soft, subtly coloured lights lit the restaurant, picking out here and there the umbrellas of leaves on the trees, the dramatic splash of the colourful plants which tumbled over the sides of ornamental urns in wrought-iron stands.

It was a perfect night, the candles on the tables flickering only occasionally in a warm and welcome breeze. From a clear and black velvet sky, the moon and her entourage of stars looked down at the scene. The night was indeed perfect, and Helen glanced down at the solitary rose in a crystal glass on the table, knowing a sadness which was almost painful.

'Helen?'

She looked up to see Scot's glass raised in a toast. They were drinking champagne, cold and sparkling and delicious. It was unlike any other champagne Helen had tasted—but this was vintage, imported from France.

'To your eyes, my darling,' he said quietly. 'And to our next meeting. Please God it won't be long.'

She drank, silently echoing his last sentence. Her mind raced ahead in time, wondering when she would see him . . . *when*?

'What is it, Helen?' he asked.

'I—was just wondering what you'll do with yourself when you live in England. From what you said about having a studio in your house, it doesn't sound as though you're planning to retire.'

'It crossed my mind. But to be realistic, I don't think I could give up my work. The composing side of it, that is,' he added quickly. 'What I mean is that I shall continue to write music, lyrics, until the day comes when I have nothing more to offer.' He smiled, shrugging. 'I don't think I can stop myself, it's too much a part of me. But I shan't perform in public in any context, that's for sure. I will value the anonymity England has to offer—which is one of the reasons I'm moving there. I shall keep strictly, very strictly, out of the limelight. No more chat shows, no more tours, radio broadcasts or interviews. Nothing.'

'Have you been back to England at all, Scot?' asked Helen.

'Twice. The last time was to visit my brother and his family.'

When she was silent, he said, 'Why do you ask?'

'It had occurred to me you might be disappointed. I mean, after all these years. . . . I thought there might be an element of—I mean, you might be associating the country with a happy childhood or something and——'

'Finding everything changed. Disillusionment? No, I'm absolutely certain about what I'm doing, what I want. I know I'll settle there. I'll make a decent home, a proper home, for Samantha and——' He broke off, reaching for her hands, his eyes suddenly intense, almost troubled. 'Helen, I know that——'

'Hey, Maestro! What the hell are you doing here, you old dog!' A chubby, beringed hand suddenly fell on to Scot's shoulder, appearing as if from nowhere and belonging to a rotund and balding man in a loud checked suit.

Helen looked up at the stranger and hated him on sight.

He was patting Scot's shoulder now, obviously delighted to see him, and Scot cursed under his breath. 'Keep your voice down, Harry. And can't you see that I'm busy?'

It was only then that the man seemed to notice that Helen existed. Eyes which denoted an excess of drinking flicked over her rapidly, then a polite but false smile touched his lips.

'Hey, I'm sorry!' He nodded towards Helen in an apologetic manner. 'I've been trying to contact you, Maestro. When're you gonna be in New York?'

'I don't know,' Scot said brusquely. 'I'll give you a call next week, okay?'

'Okay.' With a deferential bow of his head for Helen, he started to walk away.

Scot called him back. 'You didn't see me here just now, Harry.'

Harry's eyes went dirctly to Helen. 'Sure, Scot, sure. I understand!'

Helen was furious. It was patently obvious that the man had *mis*understood. 'I don't think you do, Mr . . .' She looked at him steadily. 'Scot is on holiday here *with his daughter* and his main concern is that they are not seized upon by reporters and such like. *That* is why what you're seeing right now is a mirage!'

The man's mouth opened and closed. He looked blankly at Scot, blankly at Helen, and then bade them goodnight, muttering something which included the word 'English' as he walked away.

Scot exploded with laughter, drawing attention to himself without realising he was doing so. The deep, rumbling tones he was emitting caused several heads to turn in his direction.

'Oh, dammit,' sighed Helen wearily. 'What have I done? Don't tell me *he's* a reporter? One who would respect your privacy, perhaps?'

'There's no such animal,' said Scot, when he could manage to speak.

'Then who is he? He's sitting over there now,' she added, watching as the man joined three other people at a centre table.

Scot's eyes were bright with amusement. 'Oh, nobody in particular,' he said with a shrug. 'Just a film director I've known for several years! A friend, of sorts.'

Helen flushed as she looked up at the sky. 'Oh, God!'

She groaned and then immediately asserted herself. 'Well, I don't care! He had no right to assume——'

'I don't care, either,' Scot assured her. 'And no, he hadn't.' He reached for her hand. 'Come on, my darling, let's get out of here.'

He gave Harry a wave as they left the restaurant, and Helen looked at the man with an impassive face. He looked back at her with his thoughts almost written in his eyes.

She did something she had stealthily avoided doing when they got back to the inn. She had avoided being alone with Scot in either her room or his during the time they had been in Florida. Tonight, however, when he took the key from her hand and opened her bedroom door for her, asking whether she was going to invite him in for a nightcap, she said yes.

It was several seconds before she remembered that the small refrigerators in the rooms were stocked only with soft drinks. As she walked in ahead of Scot, her eyes went immediately to the double bed. Its presence made all the difference in the world. Of course she had spent many, many hours alone with Scot at the villa, but—but not in their bedrooms.

She was tense, not only because the bed seemed suddenly to dominate the room but also because she was aching with sadness. Their precious hours alone were almost gone; the holiday was over, all but the crying.

She had turned on the overhead light, but Scot switched it off and put the lamps on instead; the two bedside lamps and one on the television. 'I—there are only soft drinks in the fridge, Scot. I never thought to——'

'I did. I did some shopping this afternoon, while you and Sam were sleeping. I'll be back in a moment. Must check on Sam, too.'

Helen slipped into the bathroom while he was gone. She ran cold water over her hands and held them to her cheeks, grateful for the air-conditioning in the rooms. She felt hot; hot, tense and aware that she was asking for trouble.

She emerged from the bathroom to find Scot opening a bottle of champagne.

'It isn't quite of the quality we had at the restaurant,' he said, 'but it's good. And cold. Where are the glasses?'

The glasses were tumblers and Helen fetched them, finding a release from her tension in chattering about irrelevancies. 'I—they're not exactly appropriate, but they're all we have.'

Scot smiled. The champagne cork went pop and he handed it to her. 'Keep it—for luck.'

She giggled nervously and put it on the coffee table between the two armchairs. 'That man—Harry—he looked at me as if I were some sort of weirdo. Did you see?'

It was only then that she realised Scot shared some of her tension. 'Forget him,' he said, almost inaudibly. He handed her a glass of champagne. 'Let's drink to our next meeting, Helen. To our reunion. To picking up where we leave off tonight.'

She looked at him, unaware that her eyes were unusually bright, unaware of how beautiful they looked, of how much they were saying. She had taken only a sip of her drink when Scot took it from her.

He put the glasses on the table and caught her to him, pulling her tightly against him, his voice thick with emotion as he spoke. 'I hate the thought of leaving you tomorrow, Helen. I hate it.' He looked down at her, the palm of his hand cupping her chin as he searched the blueness of her eyes. 'I love you, Helen. Tell me I'm not crazy, not just imagining that you feel the same way about me.'

'Scot! Oh, Scot . . .' She was choked, unable to speak for the joy which suffused her entire being. Tears of happiness filled her eyes as her heart started beating wildly, erratically. She slid her hands around his neck, her fingers losing themselves in the thickness of his hair as she rested her head against his shoulder. 'No, darling, you're not imagining anything. I love you, I love you.'

He kissed her lightly, tenderly, his hands cool against

the warm skin of her face. He was holding back from her, keeping all passion in check, and Helen resented it. She encouraged him with her mouth, letting the tip of her tongue slide over his lips.

'Helen!' He spoke on a gasp, his chest expanding as the breath rushed into his body. But he held her at arm's length, his hands trembling slightly against her shoulder. 'Sit down, my darling. I must talk to you. This is important.'

Reluctantly she moved away from him. Scot moved his chair closer to hers, saying nothing for the moment. He seemed distracted, deep in thought as he lifted her feet from the floor, letting them rest on his thighs. She watched him, saying nothing as he pushed the high-heeled sandals from her feet, letting them fall to the floor.

Still he did not look at her, didn't speak. His right hand started to stroke the smooth skin of her shins, first one and then the other, moving lightly over her ankles, the top of her feet.

A sense of unease stole into Helen, robbing her of the happiness she had felt only minutes earlier. The unease was tinged also with the stirring of something else within her, a yearning of which she was as yet hardly aware, a yearning brought to life by the way he was stroking her. 'Scot, what is it? What's wrong?'

He snapped out of it, his eyes going directly to hers. Then he looked down at his hands, at her legs. 'Gorgeous,' he smiled. Then, remembering, he turned her ankles slightly, so he could see her inner calves. His smile broadened. 'Perfect and flawless. Brown, beautiful and flawless. When did this happen?'

'Long since—virtually overnight. Darling, what's on your mind? What's wrong?'

'Nothing—everything. Helen, I've got an extremely busy time ahead of me. I'm under contract and I've got a lot of work to produce before— What I'm trying to say is——'

'What you're trying to say is that you can't move to England until you've fulfilled your commitments. I know that. You've already mentioned that it might be autumn or it might be winter.'

Scot sighed, long and hard. 'No—yes, that's right, but what I want you to understand is that you'll hear very little from me in the meantime.'

He started stroking her again as he talked and it began to impinge on her concentration. 'I understand,' she told him. 'I don't know what you're worrying about. You'll ring me when you're coming to view your house, won't you?'

'Of course. And I'll call you the day after tomorrow, when you get home. I want to know you've got home safely. Apart from that, I'll call you when I can. But don't expect letters from me or——'

'Scot, I don't expect anything from you! I'm not a child! I don't need constantly to be——'

'As long as you know that it isn't a question of "out of sight, out of mind". I'll be thinking about you every single day.' He paused in his attentions to her legs, putting a small white card on the table beside her. 'My home address and telephone number. Use it. It will have to be up to you to write to me, to call me. Reverse the charges—now don't forget. If my answering service takes the call, it means nobody's in the house. If Bessie answers, she'll tell you where I can be contacted. It'll be a question of pot luck.'

Helen laughed at him, making light of his concern. His fingers were resting lightly now around the slender curve of her ankles. She could feel beneath her legs the solid muscles of his thighs. It had taken no more than this to arouse her, this and the very sight of him. For a few moments her mind strayed on to very different ground as he continued to talk to her. She was aware of his voice but she didn't hear the words. It only lasted a few brief moments, moments during which she took in every detail of his face, his hair, his broad shoulders, the expanse of his throat and the first hint of the blond hair covering his chest. He had loosened his tie, opened the top buttons of his shirt and——

'Helen?' A slow, wicked smile chased the tension from his face, chased the concern from his eyes.

Two spots of colour appeared on her cheeks and there was nothing in the world she could do to prevent the blush from spreading. He didn't need to be a mind-reader.

Typically, he teased her, 'Why, Helen, you're blushing!'

'Go to hell,' she muttered.

Scot threw back his head, laughing as though he would never stop. He lifted her legs and lowered them to the floor, gently, as if she were made of glass. 'The last thing you didn't hear me say was that I have something for you. Before that, I told you not to forget me when you're at home on the other side of the Atlantic.'

'Oh, Scot!' She looked at him lovingly, all laughter forgotten. 'There's no chance of that.'

He took from his pocket a long, slender box which was covered in dark blue velvet. Helen accepted it uncertainly, opening it to find a gold necklace nestling there, solid gold. It was quite heavy but not in the least ostentatious, just a series of tiny blocks of gold linked intricately together so that the necklace rippled as she lifted it from its box. The workmanship was superb. It was plain, in good taste, expensive. And it was precisely the sort of thing Helen would have chosen for herself if she could have afforded——

'Scot! I——oh, I can't accept this!'

'You don't like it? I thought——'

'Oh, darling, it's beautiful! But I can't accept a gift from you. I mean, I——'

'What nonsense! Come here.' He patted his knee. 'Helen, come *here*. Do as you're told!'

She did as she was told.

She sat on his knee, her back half turned to him as he fastened the necklace in place. 'Thank you,' she whispered. 'This is very sweet of you, and it's also clever of you, because this is just the type of thing I would choose for myself.'

She heard the smile in his voice. 'I know. You don't

go in for frills and fuss, do you, my darling? I'm glad because you'll be able to wear this every day, and when you wear it, you'll think of me. You won't be able to forget me.'

Forget him? How could he think ... She didn't get the chance to protest again. Scot's arms were around her as she twisted around on his knee, then she was cradled against him and his mouth had claimed hers, and there was no restraint in him this time, no holding back.

She returned his kiss hungrily, the pitch of her arousal lifted to a dizzying height by the erotic exploration of his mouth. His hand slid beneath her skirt, resting warmly against her thigh as he locked her tightly against his body, his thumb moving in lazy circles against her flesh, sending ripples of desire surging through her.

His mouth was trailing along the smooth skin of her neck and Helen gasped softly, her eyes coming open only to see the bed. Within minutes, she knew, she would be stretched out on that bed and she would be naked, and Scot would taste every inch of her before making her his own.

Unconsciously, she stiffened, aware only that there was a battle raging between her mind and her body. Had she not loved him so much, had he not been so deliciously expert in his attentions, her mind might have won. But her clothing had been pushed from her shoulders without her realising it; the top buttons of her dress were open and Scot's lips were burning a trail of fire over the swell of her breasts.

'Scot ...' She drew away from him, trembling, her hands pushing against his shoulders as she tried to put some distance between them. As she moved, he moved, pushing himself from the chair with one hand in an easy movement, while his other arm held on to her. Then she was lifted high into his arms and he was carrying her to the bed, and all the time he was kissing her, little kisses, tantalising kisses which covered her face and her throat.

He laid her down gently, shedding his jacket and

reaching for her even before it fell to the floor, giving her no time to think, to reason, to be sure . . .

Suddenly it was too late to reason. His hands were caressing her breasts while he kissed her with exquisite eroticism until the yearning she had known earlier became an aching, throbbing need inside her.

'Helen, I love you . . .' Scot moved to take the taut peak of her breast between his lips and she buried her fingers in his hair, urging him closer as her heart beat a wild tattoo against her ribs.

'Scot, I—I'm . . .'

'I know.' He cut off her words by bringing his mouth back to hers and, as she felt the length of his body against her, the urgency of his need, she knew there was no turning back. For him or for her. 'There's nothing to fear, my darling. Trust me, trust me . . .'

She reached for the buttons of his shirt, unfastening them with trembling fingers while he dealt deftly with the remaining buttons of her dress.

A piercing, terrified scream from the next room stilled their movements, sent them both momentarily rigid.

'Samantha . . .' Scot bowed his head in an attitude of pain. 'I must go to her.'

Helen saw compunction in his eyes as he looked at her. 'Of course, of course! Scot—darling, what is it?' Already Samantha's sobbing could be heard, a piteous, muffled sound. Helen was getting off the bed, but Scot put his hands on her shoulders.

'It's nothing to worry about. A bad dream.' He left the room swiftly, telling her by his action that she should stay where she was.

Dear God, the child was so upset! Helen quickly put her clothing in order, compelled to go to Samantha.

She stopped in the doorway to Sam's room. Scot was rocking the child gently backwards and forwards, soothing her with his words, just as he had done to Helen that night . . . a long, long time ago.

The sight of them brought tears to her eyes, her heart almost bursting with love for them both. The child and the man. The man and his daughter. She walked quickly to the bed, needing desperately to help in comforting the child, knowing only too well how upsetting bad dreams could be.

Samantha detached herself from her father and flung herself against Helen, sobbing, speaking in snatches, saying something about the big car, a red car.

'It's gone now, it's gone now, darling. Sshh, it's gone away. It's only a dream.' But it wasn't, in fact. No sooner had Helen said the words than she realised what this was all about.

Over Samantha's head, she looked at Scot, mouthing her question without making a sound. 'The accident?'

He nodded.

When Sam called out for her father, Helen let him take over. She brought a glass of water and left it on the bedside table, signalling to Scot that she was leaving. Samantha was still sobbing, but far less hysterically.

Scot caught up with her by the door. 'Helen, what can I say? I'm——'

She put a finger over his lips. 'No, don't.' She smiled, a brave smile which was full of longing but devoid of regret. 'Not ever, remember?'

'I love you.'

'I love you, too ... Marcus. That's something I want you to remember.' She looked over at Sam. 'How often does this happen?'

'This is the third time since she left the hospital. It happened once at home and once at the villa. I—think she's re-living the car crash. She was out with a neighbour and——' He shook his head. 'It'll stop, given time.'

'I had no idea,' Helen said sadly. 'No idea. You—what a time you've had!' She laughed a little. 'On Trinini you had my nightmares and me to contend with!'

'Contend with? Ah, Helen, I'd like to do much more than that. . . .' Scot looked over his shoulder. 'I'll have to stay with her until she goes to sleep.'

'Naturally. Goodnight, Scot.'

Later, much later, Helen heard him come to her

room. She was awake, very much so, but she had turned her lights off. He spoke her name once, just once, and she made no reply. He tried the handle of her door once, just once, but Helen had locked the door.

She went to sleep with tears on her face, wishing she had had the courage to go after him.

CHAPTER NINE

HELEN tried very hard to pull herself together as she took her seat on the huge jet that was taking her back to England.

In the zip compartment of her handbag was the small white card which bore Scot's address and telephone number. In her heart there was a dull ache which she knew she would have to live with for a long time to come. In her mind there were a million memories which comprised the last four weeks of her life. And in her ears there was still the ring of Scot's parting words at the airport: 'I love you, my darling. Remember that.'

Leaving him, leaving him and Samantha, was something she wanted never to face again. But she would have to. When he visited England it would be only for a day or two and then there would be another goodbye until ... until he made his home in her country. His country.

And then what?

Dared she hope? Dared she hope that her future would lie with Scot? He had said he loved her, but he had given her nothing more to hope for.

The 747 was airborne and the stewardesses were demonstrating the lifebelt equipment, pointing out the oxygen supplies, the plane's exit doors.

How strange life was! Helen had gone to the West Indies as a pale and troubled girl whose emotions had been frozen under some fearful and nameless anaesthetic. Four weeks later she was returning to England fit and strong and ... a woman in love.

She ordered a drink from the trolley. She exchanged brief pleasantries with her neighbouring passengers. She went to the duty-free shop in the centre of the plane and bought a lighter for Geoff Mortimer, some perfume for his wife. For Howard she bought a quota of cigarettes and for herself she got a bottle of duty-free brandy.

As time moved on, Helen closed her eyes and tried to sleep. She couldn't. She was thinking of Scot, Scot flying west while she flew east, putting thousands of miles between them. As she got nearer and nearer to home, the passing of the miles thrust her back into reality, making the past four weeks seem almost like one long dream.

She felt this even more so when she stepped out of the airport building in London. It was nine-thirty in the morning and she hadn't slept a wink. A fine drizzle was falling and the morning was grey. As she rode along the M4 in a taxi, she took in all there was to see around her, unsure now whether *this* was the dream. The motorway signs seemed strange and yet familiar to her; it felt odd riding on the left instead of the right. As she got away from London and nearer to Reading, she looked at the lush greenery around her without experiencing a sense of pleasure at being home, something she'd always felt on returning from other holidays.

Everything looked drab and colourless. Even the village in which she lived, thronged though it was with Friday morning shoppers, seemed to have lost its prettiness and interest. Helen told herself she was just tired. Of course she was, but that was not the reason for her gloom. England was just as it always had been; it was simply that she didn't want to be here—because Scot wasn't here.

Despite the fact that it would be June in a couple of days, the house felt very cold as she stepped inside it. She picked up a pile of post from the floor, seeing at a glance that there were several brown envelopes among it—bills. She put the heating on, she put the kettle on and she looked at her watch. Scot would have got home long since. He knew what time his plane got in, local time. He would ring her soon, as promised.

Dear lord, the house looked drab! It was not only in need of decorating but the carpets needed cleaning, too.

She should have seen that months ago and done something about it. And evidence of the burglary was all around her, in every room. Corinne had done what she could in a short space of time, but there was still a little tidying up to be done—and a great deal of cleaning. She would have to ring the police, too, and see whether there was any news of her mother's engagement and wedding rings. There would also be the insurance claim to deal with, and the repair to the fridge door——

She groaned. She had forgotten the broken door when she had hastily shopped for a few groceries at the corner shop, leaving the taxi ticking over outside. Well, perhaps everything would keep for a couple of days—it wasn't warm indoors even now the heating was full on. At least, that was how it felt to her.

Two hours later she looked at her watch for the hundredth time. Had Scot and Sam got home safely? There was always that doubt where planes were concerned.

Helen's eyelids were drooping, but she wouldn't give in to it and go to bed yet, not until she'd spoken to Scot. When she slept, she would sleep, deeply, she knew.

She would sell the house. She would decorate one room, just the living room, herself, and she would have all the carpets cleaned professionally. This place was too big for her; as she moved restlessly from room to room she felt like a pea rattling around in a tin can. She would discuss it with her brother, of course, since it was his house as much as it was hers. But Howard had already told her she could do with it as she wished. She would get a two-bedroom flat, something nearer to London, so if Howard decided to come south again after finishing university, there would be a room for him. Well, the flat would be in their joint names.

When it got to nine o'clock in the evening, she knew she would have to go to bed. She was dead on her feet, almost falling asleep as she sorted out the washing.

What time was it in Los Angles? One in the afternoon. The time difference was eight hours, wasn't it? Or was it seven, now that England was in summertime? Or nine? Whatever—Scot had had all morning, American time, to ring her. But he hadn't.

Maybe he never would.

Helen checked the thought instantly. Of course he would. He was probably still in bed, recovering from his journey, if he had any sense. He would ring her soon.

The telephone woke her. There was an extension right by her bed, but even so, it was a long time before she heard it. Or rather, a long time before the noise permeated her brain well enough to tell her what the ringing meant. She snatched at the receiver as soon as this happened, dragging herself into an upright position. 'Scot?'

It was Howard.

Helen heard his familiar laugh, and the, 'Eh? What did you just say, Helen?' He didn't give her time to answer. 'So you're back! Where have you been, who with, how long for, and how are you?'

'Hello, Howard,' she laughed sleepily. 'Not now, I can't possibly tell you everything over the phone. All will be revealed when I see you. I'm in bed at the moment. I only got back yesterday morning.'

She was pleased to hear from him, very much so, and she was smiling now. But her eyes were on her bedside clock. It was noon. It was noon and it was Saturday. And Scot hadn't phoned.

'Well, I gave up ringing you last week,' Howard was saying. 'Your letter didn't tell me a thing! I'm coming home for the weekend, does that suit? Next Friday. Friday evening till Monday morning.'

'Lovely!' Helen's first thought was about what kind of roast she would give him on the Sunday. 'Friday evening? What time shall I expect you? ... Okay, see you then. 'Bye, love.' And with that, she went back to sleep for a bit longer.

By Sunday Helen's body clock had more or less

sorted itself out. She ate lunch at two, after which she took from her handbag Scot's card, the jewellers' box which came with her necklace and the champagne cork she had kept for luck. She fetched her gold necklace and lined up all these items on the coffee table in front of the settee. She hadn't got a single photograph of him. Neither he nor she had taken a camera to Trinini and the photographs which had been taken by a professional at Disney World, Sam had.

Helen looked at everything in turn and picked up Scot's card. Beverly Hills ... he probably lived in one of those palatial houses with a high brick wall surrounding it. Or was it in Hollywood, where all the houses are like that?

At four o'clock she made up her mind to ring him. She would keep it brief—and light ... 'Hi!' she would say, 'just checking that you got back all right.' She would not point out that he had let her down by not ringing. But she was let down. She had not forgotten his telling her that she would not expect to hear much from him; she understood that, and his reasons, but he had promised this one particular call, and had been quite positive about it.

The telephone rang just as she was about to pick it up, and her hand jerked away from it nervously. It was Scot, it had to be! She laughed at herself for the way her nerves started tingling in excitement. Just as she picked up the receiver, it occurred to her that it might be her boss, Geoffrey Mortimer, but she had phoned him yesterday to tell him to expect her in work on Monday. He had no reason to ring her.

It was Corinne Clayman.

Disappointment washed over Helen like a cold, black wave, only to be instantly dispelled as she realised that Corinne had been back in L.A. for days, and she might well be with Scot. Maybe she was saying a quick hello before handing the phone to him.

'Corinne! How lovely to hear from you. Are you well? Did you have a good trip back to America?'

The warmth of Corinne's personality reached across the miles. She chatted to Helen about her trip, about Trinini, about how Scot had told her about the lovely time he and Sam had had with Helen.

'You're with him now, are you?' Helen asked when she could wait no longer. 'I—may I speak to him, please?'

'Well, that's why I'm calling,' Corinne explained, 'I've just put him on a plane to New York and he's anxious to know that all's well with you. He said he was about to call you yesterday when he suddenly remembered the time difference and realised it would be the middle of the night in England! A bit awkward, isn't it . . .?'

'Yes, I—suppose so. When will he be back from New York?'

'Not till Friday.' Corinne sounded apologetic. 'Things are very hectic for him just now, Helen. I hope you'll understand.'

'Of course.' She had run out of things to say.

'Anyhow, he's calling me tonight, so what can I tell him?'

He was ringing Corinne tonight? Then why couldn't he ring England? If he could spare the time to . . . no, he had to ring Corinne on business, of course. That was different, necessary.

'Er—just tell him I . . .' Helen had been about to say just tell him I love him. But how much had he told Corinne? Had he told her he loved Helen? That when he came to England they would be picking up from where they left off in . . . yes, those had been Scot's words. But what did they mean, exactly?

'Just tell him I'm well, getting back into the old routine, you know.' As she hung up, Helen thought about that. She wasn't back in the old routine just yet—but Scot was. He was already deeply involved in his work, in his own world.

It occurred to her also after she had hung up that she should have given Corinne the telephone number of the gallery where she worked. She hadn't given it to Scot,

How *stupid* of her! This meant that the hours during which he could reach her were limited.

Helen's old routine was resumed soon enough and she felt an undeniable resentment at having to go back to work. Oh, she liked her job well enough. It was just that she knew she was incommunicado there as far as Scot was concerned.

Her resentment lessened as her first day went on, however. Geoff Mortimer told her she looked fabulous, his wife raved about her suntan—and the necklace she was wearing, and they were both genuinely pleased to see her looking and feeling so well.

Over the first few days, in bits and pieces, Helen told them her story as it all had happened—about the burglary, about Corinne turning up, about Corinne's kindness, the trip to Trinini and what it was like. And about Disney World.

She told the other members of staff, too. There were two of them and they each worked part time, depending on how busy things were and what suited everyone concerned. But she did not say a word about Scot.

To tell them about Scot would necessitate explaining why she hadn't heard from the man who loved her, the man she loved. Even if she mentioned him as Marcus Scot, questions would be asked. It was all too complicated. Better to say nothing at all. Besides, it was all too personal.

In fact, Helen would never have needed to think about whether or not she should say anything if Geoff Mortimer hadn't teased her by saying, 'Who's the man? There's something about you, Helen. You haven't merely got over your trauma—there's something else. Did you really buy that necklace yourself?'

She had considered at that point whether or not to tell Geoff—to tell anyone other than Howard, but it wasn't as if her story could end with something positive. It wasn't as if that necklace, lovely though it was, actually symbolised something. She wasn't, technically, committed to Scot in some way ... Nor he to her.

Indeed, for all she knew, that necklace might have been a parting gift . . .

That was a thought which she pushed to the back of her mind, and by Friday evening she was hopeful all over again. Scot would be home from New York today; maybe he would ring her tonight. If he didn't, she would ring him . . . probably.

Howard arrived only twenty minutes later than he'd said he would, which wasn't bad considering he had taken two trains and a taxi. He told her all his news over dinner, including the fact that he had started writing off for jobs, and when the washing up was done, Helen told him her story. It took hours, because she told her brother everything. Well, almost everything!

Howard was a year older than she. Like Helen, he was dark-haired and blue-eyed, and no one could mistake them as being anything other than brother and sister. His personality was far more forceful, though, and he was ambitious, whereas Helen never had been. But he did not lack sensitivity and understanding, and she very much wanted to hear what he had to say about Scot.

He had asked several questions during the course of their conversation, and Helen looked at him expectantly when she had brought him right up to date. She was not prepared for what he said, however.

'Well, I feel sorry for you, Helen.'

Her heart sank. 'What—what do you mean?'

'I mean now that it's finally happened to you, why did you have to fall in love with someone like that?'

'Someone like that?' She spoke with a mixture of indignation and annoyance.

'I mean there can't be any future in it.' Howard went on. 'You're going to end up hurt, Helen—I can see it coming. You're already upset because he hasn't phoned you. Be realistic, a man like that—all he wanted was an affair!'

'No!' She was sitting in an armchair with her legs curled under her and she folded her arms now, shaking her head vehemently in rejection of what she had just been told. 'That isn't true, Howard!'

Her brother looked surprised by her outburst. As if in an effort to soften the blow, he said, 'I didn't accuse you of being a one-night stand—to use his own expression. I said he wanted an affair, one that lasted a month, in this case. And that suited you, too, from what I can gather.'

'You've got it all wrong! I did *not* go to bed with him, have you got that? We did *not* have an affair. You should know me better than that!'

Howard held up a hand. 'Will you please calm down? I'm not getting at you, for heaven's sake! You're a big girl now and you don't have to answer to anyone—least of all me. I'm no angel. You wanted my opinion and I'm giving it to you. All I'm saying is that you mustn't be surprised if you don't hear from him again.'

Helen's reaction to that remark was almost aggressive, so much so that she realised it was a defence against the doubts which had been growing in her mind for the past week. 'Of course I'll hear from him! Now give me your opinion, bearing in mind that I didn't sleep with him.'

'I'll bet that wasn't for his lack of trying . . .'

'Howard——'

'All right, all right.' He shrugged. 'My opinion's the same in any case. You mustn't be surprised if——'

'But why? *Why* do you say that?'

Howard looked at her, he just looked at her. 'Wow, you have got it bad, haven't you? Before I say anything else, answer me this. Whose side am I on?'

Helen sighed. 'Mine, of course.'

'And don't forget it. This is a discussion, not an argument. I don't want to see you hurt. You're already depressed. And Scot Montague has probably left a thousand other women feeling the same way.'

She had to defend Scot. This wasn't fair. 'Don't let your opinion be coloured by what I told you about his past—by what he told me about his past. He's changed. I don't think you were listening properly. There's a lot of depth to that man and he——'

'And he's a nice person, basically. I don't doubt that, Helen.' Howard meant what he was saying, she could see that. And of course she was on her side.

She bore that in mind as he went on. 'He's also rich, good-looking—and famous. I've no doubt he's loved by many women . . . in one way or another. Okay, he said you were a real person—which simply means you were a novelty to him. He could talk to you, and I don't doubt he thought you were a sweet and lovely girl. Which you are. You're also very naïve. I think your refusal to fall into his arms like other women do was even more of a novelty to him. . . . And it's my guess that your refusal made him all the more determined. But that's your business. You've told me as much as you want to tell me.'

Helen looked down at the carpet. Howard was implying in all this that Scot's declaration of love had had ulterior motives. Scot knew she was not awed by his money or his fame. So had he asked himself what a girl such as she would be impressed by? Those three little words, for example?

No, it was too horrible to contemplate. Scot had no reason on earth to lie to her, to be false. She rejected the implication absolutely. Futhermore, she voiced it. 'If you're saying he told me he loved me as a tactic for getting me into bed, you're wrong. And you think that that's where we ended up, don't you? Wrong again, Howard. I haven't lied to you. And Scot did not lie to me.'

Howard considered her for a long time before he answered. 'Then good luck, Helen. I hope everything turns out as you want it to. And it's very obvious what you're hoping for.'

Helen floundered at that. He'd given her a short answer after long consideration. There was a great deal more he could have said, but he wasn't going to. He had decided not to. For the first time in years, for the first time since they had been adult, she felt a breach in her ability to communicate with her brother.

As if reading her mind, Howard said, 'This is my way

of avoiding an argument with you, Helen. There's no point in holding a post-mortem. So we'll change the subject now, we'll talk about selling the house. Because as far as Scot's concerned, only time will tell.'

Helen thought about that conversation after she and her brother had gone to bed. It had disturbed her enormously, and she got out of bed to fetch Scot's card. Then she phoned him from her bedroom.

His answering service came on the line, telling her there was no one at home in the 'Montague residence'. Could they take a message? she was asked. Helen said no.

She put down the receiver and picked up her clock, setting it so she would wake early in the morning, then she would ring Scot when it would be ten at night in Los Angeles.

This time, his housekeeper answered. Her voice was sleepy, and Helen realised that the woman must have been in bed already. 'Is that Bessie . . .? I'm sorry, I don't know your surname. And I'm very sorry to wake you. My name is Helen Good and I'm ringing from England. I'm—a friend of Scot's. Is he—is he back from New York?'

'Oh, yes, miss. He came to see Samantha earlier. But he's sleeping at his apartment tonight.'

'His apartment?'

'In town, near the recording studios. He usually does that when he has an early start there. Shall I give you the number?'

'Er . . . no, that's okay. I'll—ring again. If you'll just tell him that I phoned.'

Helen put the phone down. She had been taken aback; Scot had never mentioned that he kept an apartment in town . . .

She was thinking of all that Howard had said now—which was why she wouldn't ring Scot at his apartment. Because—well, did he really keep a second home because it was handy for the studios? Or because there was no housekeeper and six-year-old daughter around?

'Damn you, Howard!' she said aloud. 'Damn you for putting those sort of doubts in my mind!'

She thumped her pillow, instantly retracting what she'd just said. Howard had had good grounds—she was just remembering that she *had* ended up in bed with Scot. She squirmed a little as she got under the blankets. 'No, get it right, Helen. You were on it but not in it. There's a big difference . . .'

CHAPTER TEN

TIME told her nothing, nothing at all. Two weeks, two more weeks, passed and still there was not a word from Scot.

Helen had telephoned him twice since her first call and she was hesitant to ring again. On both occasions his housekeeper had answered and said that Scot was out, rehearsing, and unable to be contacted.

She tried very hard to bear in mind that he had warned her what to expect, or rather what not to expect. No letters, just an occasional call. But he had not even phoned her once and surely, surely in three weeks he had had half an hour to spare? Fifteen minutes? Five?

During these awful days of waiting, she had decorated the living room in her spare time. The carpets had been cleaned and there was a For Sale sign standing in the front garden.

At the end of this third week, during the weekend, Helen picked up the telephone receiver several times—only to put it back on its cradle. The last thing she wanted was to make a nuisance of herself when Scot was so busy, or to make a fool of herself if——

Her own cynicism pulled her up short. Make a fool of herself? Scot loved her; she would not be foolish in his eyes. She must stop doubting, she really must stop doubting.

She phoned him on the Sunday. She picked her time carefully, deliberately, ringing when it would be about six a.m. in Los Angeles, in the hope that she would catch Scot before he started his day's work. And it was Sunday. Surely she would reach him this time?

The voice at the other end of the line was surprisingly lively considering the time of day. It was that of the housekeeper again.

'Bessie? I—it's Helen Good. It—I'm sorry to wake you, but I thought I'd try to catch Scot before he starts work . . .'

There was laughter, friendly laughter. 'I'll ask him to call you back when he *finishes* work. He's been in his studio here all night and it's more than my job's worth to disturb him. But he'll come up for food sooner or later.'

'You mean—he's worked through the night?'

'He often does,' said Bessie, as if she were resigned to her employer's eccentricities. 'Works all night and sleeps all day sometimes. He says you can't create to order, nine to five.'

'I . . . see. Yes, quite. Well, I—I'll . . .'

The housekeeper took pity on her. 'Has he not called you back yet, miss? I did give him your messages, but he's got so much on at the moment . . .'

Now Bessie was reassuring her, just as Corinne had, and Helen began to feel like a nuisance. 'Yes, of course. Er—well, I'll ring another time.'

She was just about to hang up when Bessie called to her. 'Miss Good? Miss? Are you there? . . . Samantha's just come in. I'm in the kitchen, by the way, you didn't wake me. She wants a word with you . . .'

Sam greeted Helen with one of her long sentences. 'It's me, Helen—hello I know you called before but I didn't know then and I asked Bessie if I could talk to you if you called again.'

Helen's spirits soared. Sam had not forgotten her! 'Hello, darling! How are you? Are you still nice and brown?'

'Course! Aren't you?'

'Not as much. I'll have to stop washing because it's wearing it off.'

Samantha was highly amused. 'Haven't you got any sunshine there?'

'Not much.'

'We've got lots and I've been in our swimming pool every day. But it's not as good as the sea, but Daddy hasn't got time to take me to the beach.'

That was as far as Sam's news went, and Helen hung up feeling considerably better. Two hours later, Scott phoned.

But a curious thing happened.

Helen found herself stuck for words. It was as if time and distance had eroded all spontaneity. Or maybe it was just that she had so much to say, she didn't know how to begin.

On hearing his voice, her heart started beating like a mad thing, her hands trembling as she held the receiver far more tightly than was necessary. 'Scot? I—how are you?'

Her eyes closed with relief as he plunged into an apology and an explanation. Fortunately, he wasn't stricken by nervousness. 'I'm dead beat, my darling, but I'll survive. I put myself in a difficult position by taking so much time off with Sam. But it was worth it,' he added quietly, and she could almost see him smiling.

Helen kept her eyes closed, visualising his face. Everything was all right! Why had she ever doubted him? She felt guilty, and she was choked with emotions, happiness. Oh, it was so good to hear his voice, so *good*!

He was asking about her, and she tried to pull herself together. 'I—I'm fine, darling. Just fine. I—was getting worried about you——'

'About me?' He seemed amused. 'In what way?' Before she could answer, he said, 'That isn't what you mean at all, is it? You mean you were worried about *us*. Now listen, I want you to remember that I told you, you mustn't think that because you don't hear from me——'

'I don't,' she said hastily. 'I mean, I remember. I do remember. It's just . . .' What an idiot she was! She was crying. These past three weeks had been more of a strain than she realised. She had known doubts, so many doubts, and now that he'd actually phoned her, she could hardly speak.

'Helen? Helen, what's wrong? . . . Hold on a minute, will you? Corinne's just arrived, by the sound of it . . .'

The phone went quiet. Helen hung on for several

minutes, thinking he had forgotten her. It was only when he came back on the line that she heard tiredness in his voice. 'Helen, I'm sorry, but I'll have to go now. Corinne's here and she's having fits. I'm going on tour in two weeks and she's just had a call from the drummer I work with. He's been taken to hospital—I'll have to find out what's up. I'm sorry——'

'It's all right, Scot. I didn't know about—how long will you be on tour?'

'Only three weeks. I'll call you, Helen, just as soon as I can.'

He hung up.

Three weeks. He hadn't told her anything about a tour being part of his commitments. But then he hadn't specified what his commitments were.

Helen wrote to him there and then. The phone call had gone badly and it was his turn for some reassurance now. If she hadn't behaved so stupidly, so emotionally, she could have told him that nothing was wrong, that she loved him as she would never, ever, love anyone else.

She put it in her letter. She put her heart and soul into her letter, reminding him about little things they had laughed about in Trinini, about the ants, about playing ludo on a moonlit terrace. She kidded him about enjoying Disney World nearly as much as Samantha had, and she ended by telling him she couldn't wait to see him, that she loved him and that nothing in the world was wrong. She said on paper what she had been unable to say on the telephone, and remembered to include the phone number of the gallery and the name and address and her hours of work.

There were two weeks to go before he started his tour, more than enough time for her letter to reach him before he left Los Angeles. She posted it airmail the following day, from the big Post Office near work. As she dropped it down the chute, she told herself she must be patient now. If she heard nothing from him for a while, she must understand.

CHAPTER ELEVEN

SHE didn't hear anything. Not a word. And her doubts came back with a vengeance.

June had changed to July, and by the end of July she had accepted an offer for the house. In turn she had made an offer for a flat in Ruislip, which would make commuting to work much easier. She had spoken to Howard every weekend and he had decided he wanted no part in the flat, that he was going to stay in the north. He had been offered a job in the northern branch of a national company, and the prospects were good. As their father had willed it, they therefore shared everything he had left them, insurance money and all, splitting it down the middle, and there was enough for them each to buy their own properties.

Helen felt lonely. She had hoped that Howard would come south again. But she never faltered in her decision about selling the family home; there were too many memories haunting her there, too many reminders of what had happened to her father.

She felt she was entering a new phase in her life, going ahead with the purchase of her flat ... and it looked as though Scot was not to be part of her life, after all. He hadn't even bothered to send her a postcard.

It was the end of July. Scot would be back from his tour now, and she was thinking about him constantly. She was riddled with doubts and uncertainties—but she had not completely lost faith. She was still telling herself how busy he must be, moving around from city to city, probably. She was still telling herself he would ring and, better still, that she would see him soon. She would see him for one or two days, at least when he came to look at houses.

Howard told her in no uncertain terms that she was a

fool. He had rung her every weekend, starting the conversation with, 'Well?' And every week she had said, 'No. Nothing.'

He had restrained himself until this phone call at the end of July, making no comment to her negative answer, just showing that he was interested. But when Helen said that Scot would be home from his tour now, that he would be sure to ring her any minute, Howard let rip.

'So there was no response to your fan letter, eh? You're a bloody fool, and it's time you woke up, Helen.'

'Fan——?' She was horrified, appalled. And she gave her brother as good as she got. 'You just don't understand how it was—is—with me and Scot. I explained everything to you in detail, but you obviously missed all the finer points. I loved that man *before* I knew who he was. So don't dare talk to me as if I were a starry-eyed kid who's besotted with the idea of——'

'Then stop acting like one. Get on with your life. You've almost been living like a hermit. Go *out* in the evenings. Go out with your girl friends and stop waiting for the blasted phone to ring. It's pathetic, and I hate to think of you like this.'

'Then *don't*!' She hung up on him.

She was shaking with anger. She was also very close to tears, very close. She let out a long breath, steadying herself. Dear lord, she had never hung up on anyone before, let alone her brother. She picked up the phone and called him back. 'I'm sorry,' she said shakily, 'I shouldn't have put the phone down.'

'It's all right,' Howard spoke on a sigh. 'I am on your side, love, but you must file away that episode with Scot as a holiday romance.'

Listening to Howard shook her up. She regretted that she had laid bare her soul in that letter to Scot. Whether he meant it to be or not, his lack of response felt like an insult.

One thing was certain, she would not ring him again.

She had made all the moves so far. Enough was enough.

She went in to work the next day minus her necklace. She had worn it daily, faithfully, because Scot had wanted her to. Now, she felt idiotic about that. Besides, she didn't need a trinket to remind her of him.

A trinket?'

No. It was a gift which had been chosen with care. Scot had wanted to please her, to buy something she would have chosen herself. Or had that all been part of . . .?

She had never told Howard how close she had been to making love with Scot. She had never told him because he would only say that it proved his point. *Was* he right? Had her final evening with Scot been planned by him from start to finish—a finish with a conquest?

The evidence certainly supported the idea . . . the way Scot had wined and dined her, the champagne, more champagne in her room, a gift, a speech and a declaration of love . . .

No. No! Howard was wrong, he was *wrong*!

Corinne Clayman phoned the following Sunday. It was the first Sunday in August and, according to Helen's reckoning, Scot had been home for a week.

She was just about to get into the bath when the phone rang in the middle of the evening, and she was still hoping it would be Scot. It wasn't, and as nice as it was to hear from Corinne, Helen was bitterly disappointed.

'Corinne, this is a surprise!' She couldn't think of anything else to say, she couldn't imagine why Corinne was ringing.

'Look, Helen, I was wondering if I could buy you lunch tomorrow. I'm in London.'

'In *London*?' Helen's disappointment vanished at once. This could only mean one thing: Corinne was here to look at a house for Scot! And that meant he would—'Is Scot with you?'

'No. Helen, I want to talk to you, but not on the telephone. Will you have lunch with me tomorrow?'

Helen sank into a chair. In her excitement, she had not heard the despondency in Corinne's voice. 'What's wrong? He isn't hurt or something? Oh, Corinne——'

'No, he's fine—absolutely fine. Shall we say one-thirty tomorrow. Can you come to the Dorchester?'

'Of course. But——'

Corinne cut her off apologetically. 'Forgive me, Helen. I've got a dozen calls to make. I'll explain everything tomorrow, dear. Ask for me at reception.'

Helen put the receiver down slowly. She knew, really, what this was all about. She knew, but she didn't want to believe it. Scot was not coming to England—not yet. That was what Corinne was going to explain . . .

The following day she told her boss she would be taking a long break for lunch and that he should expect her when he saw her.

When she got to the Dorchester, the receptionist announced that Helen was expected and would she please go up to Mrs Clayman's suite. Helen did so, her heart growing heavier by the minute. Why hadn't Corinne met her in the bar or the restaurant? Why this need for privacy?

'Helen, it's lovely to see you! Come in, come in.' Corinne greeted her with a hug, with enthusiasm and a warm smile. She looked beautiful. She was perfectly made up and immaculate in a brown silk shift which was the same colour as her eyes and the perfect foil for her light blonde hair. A very tall, elegant woman.

The perfume she was wearing plunged Helen back in time to the night she had ridden in the chauffeur-driven car with Corinne on their way to this very same suite, to the time she had assumed she would never see this woman again, when Corinne herself had said they were just ships that passed in the night.

Despite the warmth of her greeting, it was plain to see that Corinne was uneasy and troubled. It showed in her eyes.

'Corinne, I don't want anything to eat, thank you. But I would like a drink.'

'I—yes, that's exactly how I feel. Brandy?'

Helen nodded and sat down. The best way to get this over with was to come straight out with it. 'You've asked me here to tell me that Scot isn't coming over to England, haven't you? He can't spare the time to come and look at the house. . . . I assume you've found one for him?'

Corinne took her time about answering. She handed a glass to Helen and sat down on an ornate lady's chair by the window. 'Yes, I have. I looked at a place in Oxfordshire this morning. It's just what he wants. We thought it would be when we saw the brochures and details which were sent to us. But Scot is coming to see it for himself; it's his decision, naturally. He—obviously wouldn't allow me to make it for him.'

There had been a fleeting moment when Helen thought everything was all right, after all, but the look in Corinne's eyes was telling her otherwise now. Corinne's news was, in fact, worse than Helen had anticipated. Far worse.

She lifted her head. 'Then it's—Scot doesn't want to see me. That's it, isn't it?'

'No!' Corinne moved swiftly, a look of horror on her face. She sat closer to Helen, her beautiful brown eyes widened with alarm. 'Helen, *no!* He has every intention of seeing you. And if he knew that I was talking to you like this . . . well, I daren't think about that.'

Helen stared at her. 'Then what is it? Corinne, please! You're making no sense at all. What *is* this all about?'

Corinne looked at her with something approaching compassion. 'It's just—I felt I ought to warn you that Scot's—changed. I suspect that the man you met on Trinini was . . . Well, he's himself again. And I felt I should prepare you——'

'Himself again?'

'Helen, listen to me. When Samantha had her accident, Scot was devastated. And he blamed himself for neglecting her—which is nonsense. All right, he hadn't spent as much time with Sam as he might have, but her accident had nothing to do with him. She was simply out in a car with a neighbour and two other children. It was something that could have happened at any time, anywhere. I tried very hard to convince him of that, but he continued to blame himself. He also felt guilty because he couldn't be found. At the time of the accident, he was——'

'He told me all this,' Helen interrupted. 'I know what he was doing, and I know about his guilt. I know also that he hated himself and it was during this time that he decided to emigrate. When he comes to England, he's going to concentrate solely on composing. He's going to keep out of the public eye and live a much quieter life—giving more to his daughter and his home life.'

'No.'

Helen could feel the blood draining from her face. 'What do you mean—no?'

Corinne smiled sadly—sadness that was meant for Helen alone. 'I've known him for many years, my dear. I understand his mind, his moods. I'm more to him than agent and manager——'

Helen looked up sharply. Scot had denied that there was anything between himself and Corinne, and she had believed him. But how could she be sure, now? She couldn't be sure of anything as far as Scot was concerned, not any longer . . . 'Answer me one question, Corinne. And for God's sake, tell me the truth. Are you Scot's—are you and he lovers?'

The last thing she expected was laughter. It was soft and feminine and attractive—and shortlived. It was followed by a smile which held just a hint of wistfulness. 'No, we're not lovers, nor have we ever been. Scot was twenty-four when I met him. I was twenty-eight and I'd been happily married for several years. He knew my husband well, and our relationship had always been one of business.'

'And friendship.'

'Yes, very much so. But that's all.'

'So you're not in love with him.'

Corinne looked at her as though she were a little girl who had said something silly. 'You're the one who's in love with him, not I.'

Helen looked down at the carpet.

'If I weren't aware of this,' Corinne said gently, 'I wouldn't be talking to you now, would I? I have a fair idea what Scot led you to believe, but he's already talking in terms of merely seeing how things go over here. Oh, I've no doubt he'll buy that house when he sees it, but he won't settle in England. He won't *settle* anywhere. My dear, he's thirteen years older than you—thirteeen going on a hundred, I'd say—and he's lived the kind of life you've only read about in magazines. You have no idea, really. He——'

'But he's changed! He told me he wanted to get out of that scene, to live differently from now on, that he wasn't really happy all those years.'

Corinne sighed, shrugging helplessly in the face of Helen's innocence. 'I'm afraid that's nonsense. Oh, he meant it at the time, I don't doubt, when he was upset and guilt-ridden. *That's* the man you met, my dear. He took time off to be with Sam when she came out of hospital. He ended up in Trinini with her, and I had no idea that would happen. And I feel responsible about you, Helen. This is why I felt I had to talk to you, to warn you before you see him. He's himself again. He's not the man you fell in love with ... Helen, what do you suppose he's been doing for the past two months?'

Helen looked at her numbly. 'I—fulfilling his commitments. He had this tour booked, for one thing. He had no choice——'

Patiently, Corinne said, 'And if he felt so passionately about getting out of that life, why didn't he cancel the tour?'

'Because—because he's under contract. I don't know. You tell me.'

'He could easily have cancelled it. All it would have cost him is money, and he's got plenty of that. Do you begin to see what I'm telling you? A leopard can't change its spots, Helen. He's thrown himself into his

usual lifestyle for the past two months and he's loved
every minute of it. Believe me. I've been with him. He
won't give it up for long—I know him of old. I've been
in this business many years, and these people are all the
same. They need to have their egos stroked, they need
the adoration of the public, it's like a drug to them.
And Scot is not a one-woman man——'

Helen got up. She had heard enough. She didn't need
to have the picture painted for her in minute detail. She
was thinking about Scot's apartment in town. Yes, he
had slipped back into his old routine ... in every
respect. *That* was what Corinne was trying to tell
her ...

'I—must get back to work. When—when is he
coming over?'

'I'm not sure. You see, I haven't called him to give
him an opinion about the house just yet. I only saw it
this morning—and I wanted to talk to you first. He's in
New York at the moment. He'll come over and stay the
night. Maybe tomorrow, maybe Wednesday, I don't
know yet. As soon as he hears from me, he's going to
call you.' Corinne had paled considerably, and Helen
felt almost as sorry for her as she did for herself.

'Helen, all I wanted ... I've no idea what Scot plans
on saying to you. He wouldn't confide in me to that
extent, obviously. But I just felt I should—should
prepare you to find him changed. Oh, I just don't know
whether I've done the right thing or not ...'

Somehow, Helen managed to smile. She managed it
because she had to, for Corinne's sake. 'You can stop
worrying. I did a lot of thinking after you phoned me
last night, and this is not the shock you seem to think it
is. Don't worry, Corinne. Scot will never know that this
meeting has taken place. You don't have to feel
responsible for anything, either. I should have—I could
have—left Trinini the day he arrived.'

Helen walked back to work. Of course Corinne had
not been thinking wholly of her, she was aware of that.
She might feel responsible for Helen's meeting Scot in
the first place, but her main concern, naturally enough,

was him. She had thought that preparing Helen for disappointment would make things easier for Scot, that it would smooth the way for him. After all, he was aware of the extent of Helen's feelings for him; she had put them plainly enough in her letter.

Remembering the tone of that letter was as embarrassing to Helen now as it obviously must have been to Scot when he read it. No wonder she hadn't heard a word from him since! But that was where Corinne's warning was of most help because it settled Helen's mind as to the attitude she would adopt with Scot. She would be friendly with him, but cool. She would be composed and she would be casual. It was comforting to remember that the letter had been written six weeks ago—because both Scot and Helen were aware from experience how much could happen to a person in six weeks, how much one could change.

Helen got back to work feeling slightly peculiar. Her mind and her emotions were divorced, totally at variance. She was thinking about Scot with absolute clarity, but then she had been prepared, intellectually, for losing him long before Corinne's little tête-à-tête. Emotionally, however, she was not prepared. She loved Marcus-Scot-Montague more than ever, no matter what he was or was not. She missed him more than she would ever have believed possible.

No, her heart would not accept it, but in her mind she knew he would be seeing her while he was in England this once, just this once, in order to say goodbye. That, at least, was something to be grateful for. He was doing the decent thing in facing her. And for all the world, she vowed, she would appear to be meeting him halfway.

Scot phoned that evening. Helen let the phone ring a few times before picking it up, feeling grateful again to Corinne as she did so because she had been given time to rehearse, time to compose herself.

'Helen? Hi? It's me. I'm in New York at the moment, but I'm coming to England tomorrow. I've just had a call from Corinne and it's all happening, at last!'

'Scot? Hello? This is a nice surprise, how are you?' It came out perfectly with just the right balance of surprise and detachment.

'Fighting fit.' There was a pause, a very slight pause, before he went on. 'How are you?'

'Oh, I'm fine, thanks. Working hard but enjoying it, you know. Life's pretty good at the moment.'

It was there again, a fleeting hesitation. 'Can you meet me at the airport tomorrow morning? You're not far from Heathrow, are you? I'll be in at eleven, your time.'

'Tomorrow? No, I don't live far, but—Scot, this is very short notice. For one thing, I don't have a car, and for another thing I'm working tomorrow.'

There was no hesitation this time. 'Working? But surely you can ... Helen, I'm only staying one night. That's all I can manage. Take the day off work. Tell them you're sick or something, can't you?'

'Well, I suppose——' She let her voice trail off. She closed her eyes. She was not holding the receiver too tightly and she was calm inside. Astonishingly calm. She had anticipated all sorts of contingencies, including this one, and she knew exactly what she was going to suggest to Scot.

'Helen?'

'Sorry, I was just thinking how I can work things out. Let me see ... you're taking a flight from New York tonight. Of course, it's already eight in the evening here, but I could ring my boss at home ... yes, all right. You'll have a car waiting for you at the airport, I suppose?'

'Of course. I'll drive to your place. Give me the directions from the airport, I'll be with you in time for lunch.'

Helen had anticipated this possibility, too, and she would not be providing lunch for him; there was no way she wanted to be alone with him and make things more difficult for herself. They would go out for lunch. She even knew where they would go.

When she asked Scot, quite deliberately, whether

Corinne would be with him, there was a lengthy pause before he answered.

'You seem to have forgotten what my plans were, Helen. Corinne is already in London. I've been leaving the house business up to her, remember? Well, she's found one. It's in Oxfordshire——'

'Really? A nice part of the country.'

'Yes. Corrie looked at it this morning, and she's been trying to reach me ever since, to tell me it's just what I'm looking for. Anyway, we can talk about this when we meet, can't we . . .'

Helen gave him the directions to her house and put the phone down. It was only then that her hands started trembling. She had coped beautifully with the phone call, with her act, and she felt nothing. Nothing at all. She was dead inside. But she couldn't seem to stop the trembling of her hands.

Geoffrey Mortimer, her boss, was just about the only thing in Helen's life that was right at the moment. He took the news that she would not be in the following day with complete understanding.

'I thought you looked peaky this afternoon,' he said.

'No, no, I'm not ill, Geoff.' Helen had no intention of lying to him. He deserved better than that. 'A friend's coming over from abroad. It's a fleeting visit and I want to see him while he's here.'

'I'll bet you do!' There was a smile in Geoff's voice. 'He wouldn't be coming from the Bahamas, by any chance? Or the States, perhaps?'

'How——'

'How did I know? Come off it, Helen! You haven't been yourself for the past few weeks. But for the first fortnight after your holiday, you were positively glowing. It doesn't take much working out, does it?' He laughed heartily, and Helen heard him say something that sounded muffled. To his wife, presumably.

She bit her lip, wishing now that she had told him she was ill.

'Kate says it must be the man who bought you the necklace,' Geoffrey went on. 'The man you've been pining for.' He was laughing goodnaturedly, having no idea how upsetting this was. 'Kate says she'll stand in for you tomorrow, and you should have a good time.'

'Geoff, you're making far too much of all this——'

'Oh, yes? Enjoy your day off! See you Wednesday.'

There was no feeling of inner calm for Helen the following morning. She woke at an ungodly hour and tried unsuccessfully to get back to sleep. She had nothing to do but stay in bed, at least until daylight came. Nothing to do but think about Scot.

As the hours ticked by she got more and more agitated. She tried to do everything at a leisurely pace to help pass the time. She did not want to see him. She had lost her nerve completely. It would have been more sensible, healthier for her, to have severed this relationship over the telephone.

She bathed and dressed with excruciating care, needing every bit of confidence which the right make-up and clothes would provide. It seemed to be getting hotter as the morning wore on. What an idiot! Of course it was getting hotter. It was August and the sun was shining. She went through the contents of her wardrobe five times before settling on a simple day dress in canary yellow. It suited her colouring very much, and it was appropriate for the hotel where they would go for lunch. Needless to say, she did not wear her gold necklace.

Oh, God! Why hadn't she thought yesterday how much better it would be to refuse to see him? It would have suited him better that way, too. He was only doing this out of good manners.

At eleven, she looked at the clock for the hundredth time before dialling the airport. His plane was due in only ten minutes later, she was told. It was circling the airport now, probably. Helen made herself some coffee, but she didn't drink it because she'd already drunk too much.

What she needed was a brandy. Scot's drive to her home would take half an hour, give or take. If she added that time to the time he would take getting through Customs, she would know exactly when to expect him. And he'd have to wait for his luggage. No, he wouldn't have luggage if he were only staying one night, just a briefcase or something. Hand luggage, that was it. That was all.

Helen's arm froze in mid-air. She looked at the brandy she had just poured into a glass and realised that this was quite the wrong thing to do. She absolutely did not want Scot to catch a whiff of brandy on her breath. Just as bad would be the possibility of her saying the wrong things as a result of alcohol on an empty stomach. If there were just something she could take which would calm her while at the same time leaving her sober . . .

The tranquillisers! They had lived at the back of her dressing table drawer ever since she'd come back from Florida. She had very nearly thrown them away. What luck that she hadn't! If ever she needed tranquillisers, it was now. She fetched them. It said on the bottle that she should take two.

She took three.

She took three and then she made herself sit down and wait. By the time Scot arrived, she was feeling . . . competent.

He pulled up in a navy blue Volvo which Helen could see from the window. She stayed where she was until he rang the door bell.

Seeing Scot came as a shock to her in spite of the fact that she had envisaged this moment countless times in the past, in spite of the fact that his face was so familiar to her.

Because it was and it wasn't.

It was a little more rugged than she remembered, and rather more good-looking, despite the signs of tiredness she could see, attributable to his journey and his pace of work. Among other things.

'Helen!' He was smiling and he was reaching for her.

'Scot. It's good to see you.' She turned her head as he went to kiss her, just enough so that it was only her cheek he kissed. Come in. Did you have a good flight?'

He answered her as they walked into the living room. Then, 'I see you've sold the house. There's a sign——'

'Yes, I've bought a flat.'

'I——see. Too many reminders here, I suppose?'

'Of my father. Yes.' She met his eyes squarely for the first time. She couldn't read what she saw in them. They were beautiful, clear and green and fringed with golden lashes a shade lighter than his hair, that thick and magnificent mane of his. He still wore it just a little too long at the back.

He was searching her eyes in that way which was so familiar to her, that way he had of trying to read what was going on inside. Fortunately, there was nothing going on inside. Thanks to the tranquillisers, Helen was physically calm. Her heart had not started jumping all over the place and there was no chance that she was wearing her emotions in her eyes.

Whatever Scot saw, it satisfied him. She saw his eyes change, but still she could not read them. Not that she needed to; she knew what he was feeling—relief, plain and simple. They were meeting as two people on whom time and distance had taken its toll. They were strangers, friendly strangers. And that suited him fine.

He asked whether he might use the bathroom in order to shave and to change, and it was only then that Helen saw he did have a suitcase with him. A small one.

She sat down and waited for him, feeling pleased with herself so far. Scot emerged from the bathroom looking more relaxed, wearing a light brown, lightweight suit and an open-necked shirt in darker brown. Yes, he was broader than she remembered, too.

On the way to lunch, she asked about Samantha and he asked about her brother and they talked almost constantly, and nothing was said. Over lunch, things became a little more awkward.

'No wine?' he queried. 'But you always enjoyed wine with your food in Trinini.'

Helen smiled and came up with the ideal answer. 'I

was on holiday then, Scot, and people behave differently when they're on holiday. I never normally drink wine during the day—it tends to make me sleepy.'

'I never noticed it having that effect on you.' He was watching her closely again.

It would have, if I'd taken three tranquillisers beforehand, she thought to herself.

'No quick repartee, Helen? And won't you have at least one glass?'

She laughed a little. 'No to both questions.' Casually, she went on, 'And what if you don't like this house in Oxfordshire? Will you keep looking, or are you likely to change your mind?'

He frowned. 'I'll keep looking, of course. Helen——' He broke off as the waiter approached with their main course.

'The food's pretty good here,' Helen said, as the waiter went away. 'It's an old hotel, as you can see, but their standards never slip behind the——'

'Helen——'

She looked at him in surprise. 'Scot! I was in midsentence! I thought that someone who had lived in the States for so many years would be interested in an old English building like this.'

He looked at her, he just looked at her and said not a word. But she had had to fend him off. The tone of his voice had been serious and she knew he'd been about to make some sort of speech. And that was the last thing she wanted. It would be too embarrassing to endure if he were to start making his excuses or explanations. Then she really would feel like a fawning fan who was being thrown a few crumbs by the maestro. And even the tranquillisers couldn't cope with *that*. For the first time in over an hour, she was ruffled, ruffled by the very thought of it.

She glanced down at the food on her plate. 'I—think I will have a glass of wine, Scot. Just the one.' She shrugged. 'I can always have a siesta this afternoon, since I've taken the day off.'

'A siesta?' That was all he said. He started eating,

and Helen followed suit, making a determined effort to clear most of the food from her plate.

She was about halfway through it before he spoke again. 'Helen, I'd thought—I was wondering whether you might like to look at the house with me. Corrie made the appointment for me for four o'clock.'

Helen looked at her watch. This was turning out to be very easy indeed—thanks to this morning's brainwave, and all the planning she had done last night, after his call. 'Oh, Scot, I'm sorry. That would have been fun, but it's too late.'

'Too late?' He obviously had no idea what she was talking about.

'Mm. I've got a date in London at seven, and by the time we'd driven to Oxfordshire and—no, I'm afraid I can't. I'd never make it in time.'

She picked up her wine and drank some of it before meeting his eyes. Lying did not come easily to her, after all, despite what she thought a moment ago. Nor was she an actress.

But Scot was convinced she was telling the truth, and that was all that mattered to her. 'You know I'm only here for one night, Helen. I—assumed we'd be having dinner together.'

Things were getting harder now. She wanted to tell him that that wasn't necessary, that he didn't need to take her to dinner as well as to lunch. Of course she would say no such thing. She was still very much in control and she was as sober as a judge.

In any case, Scot spoke before she did. 'You didn't think of cancelling this date, I suppose?'

She looked at him blankly, more blankly than she realised. 'Well, I didn't think you'd expect that of me. I mean, it isn't as if you'll be alone this evening. You said Corinne's in town. And this was all at very short notice, Scot. I don't think I could have cancelled it.'

'And you didn't want to?'

'No, actually, I didn't.'

Things got better instantly. Scot actually sat back in his chair and thus let her see how relieved he was. It was the first honest thing that had happened between them.

They reverted to small talk while they finished their meal. It was only as their plates were taken away that Helen felt slightly woozy. Stupidly, very stupidly, she had drunk two glasses of wine without realising she'd done so. The waiter had automatically topped up her glass.

The feeling passed after a moment or two, and she helped herself through it by continuing to talk. 'How did your tour go, by the way?'

'It was hectic. We worked in sixteen different cities in twenty-one days.'

'Good heavens, that's a lot of travelling. So you didn't enjoy it?'

'I didn't say that. As a matter of fact, I enjoyed it far more than I expected to.'

And there it was.

It had never occurred to Helen that Corinne might be mistaken about Scot. She was his agent, his manager and friend of many years. But if Helen had needed any further confirmation of the accuracy of Corinne's forecast—there it was.

They left the hotel ten minutes later, and it was in the car that an atmosphere began to build up, a very awkward atmosphere.

'Well,' Helen turned to him as he pulled up outside her house, 'it was lovely seeing you, Scot, I really enjoyed it. Thank you for lunch.' She glanced at her watch. 'You'll have to get a move on, won't you? Do you know the way to the house?'

'There's a map supplied with the car. Helen—I'd like to keep in touch. I'm flying back in the morning, directly to Los Angeles, and I——'

'Then I'll ring you,' she said. So he was being a gentleman to the end. Well, she would maintain her dignity to the end. They both knew this was goodbye. 'I know how busy you are, so I'll ring you. It would be nice to keep in touch.'

He even got out of the car and opened the door for

her. 'You'd better go and have your siesta before you go out on the town. That's the third or fourth time you've stifled a yawn.'

'Is it?' she laughed. 'Sorry! It's the wine, I told you! It's nothing personal.'

'Thanks,' Scot said drily. He made no attempt to give her even the most perfunctory of kisses. 'Goodbye, Helen.'

She did it. She did it with a rock-steady voice. 'Goodbye, Scot. Good luck with the house.'

When she got indoors, she was still all right. She looked at herself in the dressing table mirror, to make sure of it. She felt, and she looked, absolutely fine.

The next thing she knew, she was asleep.

CHAPTER TWELVE

THE pain hit her the next day. Hard. And it was, literally, a pain.

Helen woke up at two in the morning, and that was when it hit her. It was over. Finished. There was nothing to hold on to now, no hope remaining. Her emotions caught up with that which her common sense had known for a long time, and that was when the pain struck like a knife in the heart.

She cried then. She cried hysterically.

She didn't realise it would help a little; nobody plans to cry like that. She just did. And it helped—a little.

By five o'clock she had calmed down and had forced herself to eat something. By six o'clock she was under the shower.

When she walked into work at her usual time, she was made up more than usual, around the eyes, but nobody was fooled. In fact Geoff was a little uneasy for most of the day, and Helen felt almost sorry for him. She could imagine him going home and telling Kate how he had put his foot in it on the phone, the night before last, when he'd teased Helen about her date with her mystery man.

Helen vowed to do better for Geoff the next day, and she did. She worked hard and she stayed an hour longer than her usual finishing time. Fortunately the gallery was opening with a new exhibition of paintings by an up-and-coming German the following Monday, so she didn't have to invent extra work; life was busy.

By the end of the week she was, to all appearances, functioning normally. She even coped dispassionately with Howard when he rang.

He phoned on Saturday morning, and Helen was still in bed, pretending to herself that she was reading a magazine while she drank her morning tea. Of course she realised she was only pretending, but she had to make an effort, hadn't she? She would have to make an effort at normality for a long time to come. Until she became normal.

If such a day would dawn.

'Hello, Howard.' She did not give him a chance to say, 'Well?' as he had so many times in the past. She went on quickly but calmly, 'You can stop worrying about me now. It's all over. And before you say you told me so, I'll——'

Howard clicked his tongue. 'Helen, I was not about to say that! What do think I'm made of? I'm not surprised, true, but I am sorry. What happened?'

'On Trinini, Scot was in a state of flux,' she explained. 'I think that's the best way of describing it. He was angry with himself, he was riddled with guilt and he made promises to himself which he thought at the time he would keep. He's going ahead with his house purchase—as far as I know—but I have it on very good authority that he won't stay in England long. Or if he does, he won't stay out of the public eye. That's one promise he absolutely can't keep. All the time he's been back in America he's been working like a dog and loving every minute of it. That, he told me himself, face to face.'

She drew breath but she did not pause. 'I still will not concede to you, Howard, that I was nothing more to him than a sexual challenge, something he had to conquer for the sake of his ego or his persona or whatever. Nor will I concede that his saying he loved me was a deliberate lie. It was a mistake, that's all. You see, there was a time when I made a mistake, too, a time when I took love and gratitude and got them all mixed up. I believe Scot did the same, because he was grateful to me. He was grateful . . .

Her voice was rising. She was aware of it, but she couldn't stop. She was aware also that she had started out dispassionately but was now approaching tears. Doggedly, brokenly, she went on. 'But I soon realised I was in love with Scot and that it had nothing to do with gratitude, whereas he . . . he realised he was not in love with me but felt only gratitude. Another difference is that it took him a little longer to realise his mistake. About three days, I would guess—about as long as it took him to get back into his old routine!'

There was silence at the other end of the phone. 'Howard?'

She heard the click of a cigarette lighter, a deep inhalation of breath before her brother spoke. 'I'm here, love,' he said softly. 'And I'm inclined to think you're right, believe it or not. It sounds feasible. And now you've got that off your chest, will you tell me what's happened since I last spoke to you? You say you've spoken face to face——'

'Yes,' she said. Howard's faith in her reasoning was something of a relief to her. Maybe he didn't think her quite so foolish, after all. 'But . . . I'll keep this short, if you don't mind.' She gave him the essence of Corinne's warning of what to expect when she saw Scot. She told him how she'd used the tranquillisers to help her through her meeting with him, adding, truthfully, that she'd flushed the rest of the pills down the lavatory.

'. . . So our meeting went perfectly smoothly and I let him off the hook—a non-existent hook—with dignity, composure, a pack of lies and a performance that Dad's amateur dramatic society would have been proud of.'

'And a belly full of tranquillisers.'

'Howard——'

'I'm not saying a word. They served a purpose. As long as you have flushed——'

'I have. And while you're bound to think I'm biased, I give Scot full credit for coming to talk to me. I admire him for doing it that way. It was . . . a mark of respect . . . the residue of the gratitude he felt. I always treated him merely as a man, you see—on Trinini. He liked that. And he seemed to think I'd forgiven him for something when he told me about his past. I didn't pass judgment, you see. I just reminded him again that he's human, like the rest of us. We all get carried away from time to time—as I did when I wrote him that letter.'

'He didn't mention that, I hope?'

'Of course not!' She sighed. 'You still don't really understand him, do you? But then how could you, when you never met him? I'll admit there was a moment when I thought he might mention it, and start an explanation of some sort, but I should have known better. At that point I changed the subject, and he believed that the letter was the furthest thing from my mind.'

'What do you mean, you should have known better?'

'I mean, brother dear, that he was too tactful to mention it. That it wouldn't have helped the situation for either of us. He is tactful, you know, Howard. And kind and considerate and understanding. And you've only to listen to his music to know that he's sensitive . . .'

There was another silence. Helen had to prompt him again. 'Now what are you thinking? Out with it—I can take it.'

'I was thinking . . . I was thinking how lucky I'd be if I were to marry a girl who loves me as deeply and completely as you love Scot. And . . .'

'And?'

'And I'm sorry, but I can't believe that he is all you think he is. Because if he were, he couldn't help but love you in return. He would never let you go. Because you *are* all these things.'

'Now *there's* bias for you!' Helen felt better, much better for talking to Howard, now that he'd begun to understand more about her relationship with Scot.

Maybe she hadn't explained it well enough to him before, and maybe her failure to do that was because she had only just begun to understand everything thoroughly well herself.

She finished her conversation with Howard after talking about her removal date, and solicitors and money and removal vans. He said he would come down to help her when she moved into her flat, on the first Saturday in September.

Time passed. Slowly. Helen started packing the

contents of the house long before she needed to, or so
she thought. She soon realised it was not too soon. She
had lived all her life in the village and had never moved
house before. And there was far more to it than met the
eye. There was, she discovered, a lot of junk in the attic,
clothes she would never wear again in her wardrobe,
pots and pans she never used in the kitchen. There were
also a lot of treasures, little things, around the house.
But the ones that had been stolen were not among
them. The burglars had not been caught and she had
given up hope of retrieving her most precious
possessions, her mother's engagement and wedding
rings.

It rained cats and dogs on the day she moved. She
and Howard closed the door on the family home for the
last time, then drove ahead of the removal van to the
flat in Ruislip.

She was grateful for her brother's help, but she could
in fact have managed perfectly well without him. Every
day she was getting stronger in a way which had
nothing to do with moving furniture around. She was
coping. She was healing.

But she was not forgetting. Every hour of every day
she thought of Scot, if only for a few minutes of the
hour. Yet she had, truly, let go of him—not that he had
ever been hers in the first place.

By the end of September she had decorated her
bedroom and the bathroom, and she had the flat just as
she wanted it. There had been no pleasure in the work
she had done, though. The flat didn't feel like home.
Not yet. Maybe this was due to the strangeness of the
area, the comparative newness of the property. Her
original home had been seven years older than she was.

No, six years older than she was. 'She would be
twenty-three on the first of October. She had forgotten
about her birthday.

Geoffrey Mortimer hadn't forgotten it. He and Kate
took Helen out to dinner that evening. They went
straight from work, in the West End. It was a chilly
evening and the nights were drawing in. It would soon

be time to put the clocks back. *Spring forward, Fall back*, an American customer had once told her, by way of an aide-mémoire. Helen had always remembered, after being told that. Still, she had to think hard when converting the time in countries of a different latitude, as she had had to when ringing Scot. Or rather, when trying to ...

On the night of her birthday, long after she had got into bed, she was unable to get Scot out of her mind, for some reason. Not that he was ever far from her thoughts. But this night she found herself hurting not for herself, but for him. He was back on the crest of his wave, at the zenith of his career. And she hoped, she hoped very much, that he was truly happy, deep down inside.

In November she went to stay with Howard for a few days, in the middle of the month. She didn't particularly want to; she felt that she ought to. She ought to show willing to make the journey, as he always had been glad to visit her, and to see his new home.

Those few days turned out to be better than expected, however, because Howard introduced her to his latest girl-friend, who had lasted a record time as far as Helen knew ... all of five weeks. And a very likeable girl she was, even if she did talk incessantly!

It was on the way back to London, on the train, that Helen spotted the newspaper article about Scot. It wasn't in her own paper that she saw it. A passenger who had got off the train at Watford had left his paper on his seat. Helen didn't have any reading matter with her; she had been looking out of the window for most of the journey south, not that she could see anything. It was late on a Tuesday evening, it was dark outside and it was raining. Helen had had Monday and Tuesday off because she had worked in the art gallery for two consecutive Saturdays, standing in for one of the part-timers who was on holiday.

The movement of the train had lulled her into a state of lethargy, and it was lethargically that she reached for the abandoned newspaper.

The photograph of Scot jumped out at her immediately she glanced at the page it was on. It was a very poor reproduction of him, and Corinne and Samantha, and there were several people in the background.

Her eyes moved swiftly to the bold print which was the heading of the article: *Expatriate Comes Home After 25 Years in U.S.A.* The article read:

'Mr Scot Montague flew in to Britain last night, and it is here that he is making his home after emigrating to the United States twenty-five years ago. While his is a household name in America, the titles of his songs will be more familiar to our readers. For he is the man who wrote "Girl Child", "Grey is the Day", "Come to me at Sunset" and many more. His most popular instrumental composition was "Lady Love", the theme from a Hollywood film which was a big box office success three years ago.

Scot Montague is known to his friends as "the maestro", says Mrs Corinne Clayman, his agent and manager. Mrs Clayman, thirty-five, an attractive American widow who has known Montague for many years, is here with him at Heathrow Airport where she had waited for the arrival of her client and his six-year-old daughter, Samantha. "I flew to England ahead of Scot," she told us, "and my first task will be to see him settled in his new home."

She was referring to Montague's estate near Clifton Hampden in Oxfordshire and said, "Life has been hectic for Scot since he bought the house, and it has stood empty ever since."

Mr Montague and Mrs Clayman will continue to work hand in hand as agent and client. She told us she is currently negotiating contracts for him in Britain, which will include several TV appearances and a tour of our islands. She refused to divulge further details, however, and said that the maestro will be resting for his first few weeks in England, adding, "Our first priority will be furnishing and decorating the house."

Mr Montague, thirty-six, is now at the peak of his career. Earlier this year he won an Academy Award . . .'

Helen put the paper down. She smiled humourlessly because Corinne had mysteriously lost five years off her age in the article. But that was the only inaccuracy it contained, and her long-range forecast of Scot's life had been correct in every respect.

She turned her attention back to the nothingness beyond the window.

The train pulled in to Euston Station shortly after ten and Helen stepped from its warmth to the coldness of the damp November night. She pulled her coat more closely around her, picked up her case and headed for the escalator to the Underground.

She felt the cold more fiercely as she walked through the freezing drizzle of Ruislip, but it was as quick to walk to the flat as it would be to wait for a taxi. As she walked, she was trying to remember what she had in the fridge; she was not only shivering but hungry and longing for a cup of tea.

There were several vehicles parked in the driveway to the building in which she lived, a sight so familiar and normal that she didn't even notice them until a car door suddenly opened a few yards ahead of her.

A man stepped out of the driver's seat, a tall, broad man, and Helen stopped dead in her tracks, facing him from a distance of three or four paces. The suitcase dropped from her hand and hit the wet ground with a dull thud.

The man was easily recognisable in the amber light cast by the street lamp, and he was far more than familiar to her, far more than dear to her. She stared at him nonetheless with something approaching terror in her eyes, because there had been no warning this time, no preparation at all. Nor had she primed herself with tranquillisers, or planned and rehearsed for this possibility. *There had been no possibility.*

She went to pieces.

There, in a public place, in the miserable drizzle, within sight and earshot of several passers-by, Helen Good went to pieces.

She had been doing so well, so very well, for such a long time. Getting better and better. The invisible, emotional wound had been healing, knitting together with the passing of each and every day.

But the very sight of Scot Montague standing before her was enough, more than enough, to rip that wound wide open. And from it, from Helen, poured all the pain, all the longing and the hurt which she had thought she had exorcised for ever. 'Get away from me!' she screamed at him. 'Get *out* of my sight, Scot, out of my life! I don't want to talk to you, I don't want to see you, I don't want to think of you ever again!'

She slumped against a car, burying her face in her hands, unable to say anything further as a sea of humiliation swept over her. She kept her head bowed, her body going rigid as Scot's arms came around her.

He smoothed her hair with his hand, his deep voice familiar and unfamiliar as he spoke. 'Thank you, my darling, for telling me what I wanted to hear. I love, you, too, Helen. My beautiful, beautiful girl . . .'

CHAPTER THIRTEEN

EXHAUSTED, confused and frightened, Helen could not believe what she had heard. She didn't want to believe it, not if it weren't real, not if it meant more pain and longing, more——

Scot loosened his hold on her, pulling her head gently against his shoulder. He held her lightly, just lightly, satisfying himself that she was steady on her feet.

She was, because she knew in that moment that he loved her, that it was true, that he had loved her for a long, long time. He was holding her exactly the same way he had held her once before, when she had known in some dusty corner of her mind that she would never, ever, forget his gesture and all the tenderness and concern it represented.

She had been confused, upset and bewildered then, just as she was now, but that thought had pierced her mind as strongly as the horrible suspicion which was growing within her this minute. Somewhere along the line there had been a ghastly, disastrous mistake, and Corinne Clayman had made it.

'Come on, Helen, let's get you indoors.' Scot spoke not gently but authoritatively, picking up her case as he led her towards the building.

It was Scot who made her tea, shedding his hefty overcoat as soon as they got inside her flat, insisting that she sit down.

The blackness of his clothes reflected the mood which descended upon him when he started to talk to her. He sat next to her, infusing warmth into her hands as he held them in his own. 'I searched for you all afternoon and waited for you all evening, my darling. I rang every gallery in the phone book until I got a response to your name. I spoke eventually to Geoffrey Mortimer, who told me you would be in to work tomorrow. At first he refused to give me your home address, wanting to know who I was. I told him I'm the man you're going to marry, that you would be with *me* tomorrow and for the rest of your life. He laughed, muttering something, then he told me where you were and gave me your address and phone number.'

Helen heard all the words, but most of them didn't register with her. Only his second sentence made sense to her. And those words made total sense. Total and shocking. And pitiable. There had been no mistake on Corinne's part. She had deliberately robbed both Helen and Scot of a piece of their lives.

'You never got my letter, did you, Scot? It was delivered to your house but not into your hands. It was intercepted and read by Corinne, who was left in no doubt whatever that what you felt for me, I felt for you. My heart and soul were in that letter, Scot, and you never received it. My love, my longings . . . *and* the name, address and telephone number of the gallery. I'd stupidly neglected to give those to you in——'

She stopped abruptly at the look on his face. Beneath the depth of his tan he had gone grey with a fury she did not want to witness. 'Scot, please, it doesn't matter. Corinne was just wrong if she thought——'

'It matters.' The words were barely audible. He sat still for several seconds, his eyes closing of their own volition as he fought to maintain control. For Helen's sake.

After a moment he got up, swearing under his breath. From the pocket of his overcoat he took a somewhat battered newspaper. He waved it at Helen. 'God and Corinne move in mysterious ways,' he said, his face taut with anger. 'Corinne, however, makes mistakes. She doesn't make them often, but . . .' He slammed the paper against his other hand. 'Here's one! This is her *finest*! Have you read it, Helen?'

She nodded numbly. 'Purely by chance. I—I automatically assumed you'd endorsed that article.'

'*Endorsed it?* I wasn't aware that she'd spoken to the press! I wasn't even aware I'd had my photograph taken at the airport! The first I knew of this was when I happened to go out this morning to buy some papers.' He threw the newspaper furiously to the floor. 'But I'll tell you this much, Helen,' he went on, pointing to it. 'I'm glad she did that! Because if she hadn't, I wouldn't be here with you now. . . . Dear God, what a scheming, conniving bitch she is!'

Helen stared at him anxiously, feeling weak with shock. 'What—you tackled her about it?'

'Tackled her? I wiped the floor with her! She saw a side of me she's never seen in all the years she's known me!'

'What—what did she say?'

He didn't answer. There was a strange look on his face.

'Scot? Scot!'

'She argued with me. Thank God, she argued with me! Because if she hadn't, I might not have laid into her so viciously. And if I hadn't done that . . .'

Helen spoke on a sigh. 'Darling, you're not making sense.'

Scot sank into an armchair on the other side of the room, his fingers raking the hair from his forehead. 'I know—I'm sorry. Okay . . . At first, Corinne looked at me blankly. "But, Scot darling, I thought you'd be pleased!" she said. "You know it always helps to have advance publicity. It whets the appetite." I demanded to know whose appetite she was referring to and what it was that advance publicity helps.'

'And?'

'And then we fought—to put it mildly. After a while, quite suddenly, she changed her attitude completely. She went all soft on me, smiling and reasonable. She said, "Look, Scot, I know I've acted against your wishes, but let's face it, you're not going to remain anonymous here. Not for long. *Because you won't want to*, you know that as well as I. You're tired at the moment, you need a rest, that's all. But you'll be back in the swing of things in no time, and I know this. I've been having a word here and there about your future work in England. I'm only thinking of you, Scot, you know that.''

Helen was wound up like a spring. 'Go on.'

He shrugged. 'By this time I was sitting down, just looking at her. I was beginning to think she'd lost her mind. I let her go on. I said nothing, nothing at all, and eventually she stopped talking. She looked at me and I looked at her. She went white then. Something which I already knew was only just beginning to dawn on her, and she went white. She was realising that this was the end of our relationship, but that's something I'd told her a dozen times over the past few months. After Sam's accident, Corinne knew what I went through. I'd made it quite clear that when I emigrated, she would be a friend to me and nothing else, that she would be in L.A. and I'd be here.

'But she never understood it, Helen. Or rather, she never believed it. That I was going into semi-retirement, I mean. I told her and told her, but she never believed it. So, this morning, I started to ask myself *why* she'd never believed it. And the answer was obvious to me.'

It was obvious to Helen, too, but she didn't interrupt him.

'Anyhow, I was just looking at her, as I say. And I was wondering how far her scheming went, to what extent she had tried to manipulate me. And I thought immediately about you. Then I got up and I walked towards her. I don't know what she saw in my face, but she took two steps backward and she looked—strange. It confirmed my suspicions. I didn't need to ask her whether she'd talked to you.'

Helen closed her eyes. Scot had painted the scene so vividly that she could see Corinne as clearly as if she were standing in the room. She shivered. 'Corinne— what did she say about me?'

Scot turned to her. He had drifted into his own thoughts and there was a look of disgust on his face. 'Your name wasn't even mentioned, my darling. Corinne is far too clever to have volunteered anything. But she knew she'd been rumbled.'

'You mean she was petrified.'

'I don't know about that. I was calm—icy calm. I told her she had two minutes in which to collect her things and get out of my house. All I could think about at that point was finding you. But if I'd known then what she'd done with your letter——'

'I blame myself for all this.' Helen flopped against the cushions of the settee, shaking her head sadly. 'I blame myself as much as Corinne. I should never have lost faith in you, Scot. I should have trusted you and never lost faith, but . . . but my brother had put doubts in my mind long before Corinne talked to me. I did remember your telling me not expect to hear from you after you went back to work, but . . . but I found it hard to take, especially in the face of criticism from Howard. I mean, I—I couldn't ignore what he thought, not when his opinion is something I've always respected. Something I asked for, too.'

'You mustn't blame him for anything,' said Scot. 'I don't. He was on the outside looking in. I don't know what he said, but . . . well, it doesn't matter now. I'm sure he was only trying to protect you.'

Tiredly, deeply, he sighed. 'I should have given you this when we were in Florida, on our last night.'

He had got to his feet, was fishing in the pockets of his overcoat. He sat down beside Helen and handed her a small box.

It was covered in dark blue velvet, as was the box in which he had given her the necklace, and she knew what was inside it before she opened it. There on the inside of the lid was the name of the Florida jewellers from whom he had bought the necklace, It was printed in gold on oyster-coloured satin. And the engagement ring was a diamond solitaire.

Helen couldn't speak. She just looked at him, loving him, hating herself for all her doubts and thinking of all the unnecessary pain they had been through. 'Scot . . . oh, Scot!'

It was a sad exclamation and he put his arms around her. 'Don't cry now, my darling. I don't think I could take it.' He held her close, brushing his lips against her forehead. 'I wanted to propose to you in Florida. I was going to. I shopped for the ring and I bought the champagne. Then I thought no, Helen won't marry me. At least, not yet. It's too soon to ask. Give her time. I thought it would be unfair to ask you then, when I knew we couldn't be together for several months because of my commitments.'

He pulled away from her slightly, his smile rueful. 'How I wish I'd extracted a promise from you!'

'Extracted? Oh, Scot, you idiot!'

He nodded in agreement. 'I didn't know what to do. I went back to the jewellers and got the necklace because I wanted to give you something. Over dinner that night, I decided I'd ask you to marry me after all. Then we were interrupted, if you remember, and by the time we got back to the inn . . .' He broke off, laughing at himself. 'I had the ring in one pocket and the necklace in the other!'

His laughter faded. 'I was unsure what I could offer you, Helen. Months without seeing me, firstly, and then—well, it was Marcus you fell in love with. I wondered whether you could live with Scot Montague, too. And then there was Samantha. I couldn't be sure you'd want a six-year-old daughter at your age.'

He reached for her, holding her close again. 'When we were on the island, I told you that after Sam's accident, I had emerged with a sharpness and clarity of mind and purpose which would never leave me. It hasn't. Not for one minute. Meeting you was like—like some sort of reward, I thought I was being given a second chance in life.'

He shook his head slowly, his green eyes suddenly sparkling with renewed anger. 'Corinne has stolen from us two very precious things which can never be bought or replaced. Time——'

'And happiness.' Helen got to her feet. They were both in need of a drink. She poured two and handed a glass to him. 'Scot . . . darling, I'm so sorry for losing faith. But when—when there was no response to my letter, it was ... In spite of what you told me in Florida I thought—well, your lack of response said it all.'

'Stop blaming yourself, Helen. Just listen. *I* wrote to *you* after we'd spoken on the phone. I was disturbed by what you said. Or rather by how little you said. You sounded very—distressed. At first I thought you needed reassurance, so I wrote to you and gave it— plenty of it.' He looked at her, giving her time to think about this.

'But I never ... You gave the letter to Corinne to post.'

'She always mailed my letters. Just as she always sorted my mail at the house. Much of it I never saw, which suited me, it was given to my secretary who worked in the house. And it gets worse, Helen—there were two or three occasions, when we were on tour, I asked Corinne to try your number for me and call me to the phone when she got you on the line. But you were always out.'

This time his smile was one of self-derision. 'I once told you she's a formidable woman when crossed, but I never, never in a million years would have thought her capable of this! Oh, she's subtle,' he added bitterly. 'I'll have to give her that. She timed it so nicely, her asking me whether I'd heard from you. I said no, I'd had no calls from you and no reply to my letter. You see it all, don't you, Helen? She's in a league of her own ...

'She planted doubts in my mind from then on. As subtly as a snake. Just the odd remark here and there, bit by bit, on the occasions when I mentioned your name ... 'Don't be too surprised if you don't hear from Helen, Scot ... Helen's very young, you know ... Maybe she's found someone of her own age by now, and you and Trinini are just romantic memories to her ... What would a young girl like Helen want with a divorcee who's got a six-year-old daughter? Be fair, Scot! You're probably expecting too much of the girl ...' Oh, yes, she was very, very subtle! And it worked, Helen. I began to think it might be true, that that's how you felt about me. After all, it was for some of these reasons that I didn't propose to you in Florida. You *are* young. I felt I ought to give you time. So I became convinced that *this* was why you were so uptight with me on the phone. Need I go on?'

'No. Allow me. Let's see ... in time, she just happened to mention you'd probably find me—changed—when you saw me. Corinne is ... she was less subtle with me. She came straight out with a warning of what I should expect.'

Helen had not sat down again. She moved around restlessly as she re-lived for Scot the scene with Corinne in the hotel. She finished what she had to say by reminding him how he'd told her he'd enjoyed the tour.

'I said I enjoyed it more than I'd expected to,' Scot amended. 'And that was partly because I knew it was my last one and mainly because I thought I had you—us—to look forward to. Every day of it was bringing me closer to the time I'd see you. As for the idea of cancelling the tour—Corinne knew damn well that was not on. It's bad enough to do that if you're sick and have no choice, but you know what they say about the show must go on—it just wouldn't do. Apart from that, I had no wish to cause bad feeling with people I'd known for years, people who've been good to me. That's not to mention a responsibility to the public, the people who've paid money for seats. Corinne was well aware of this—all of it. *Hell!*'

He exploded with anger and Helen went to him in an effort to calm him. 'Scot, Scot, it's all right. It's all——'

'It's just as well I threw her out this morning. If I thought she was in England now, I'd find her and break her neck!'

'Scot!' He'd shot from his seat and Helen was staring at him in dismay. 'Darling, please! Don't talk like that. It's *over*. Nothing matters now except us. You're here, I'm here. I can——'

'How can you take this so calmly after what she's done to us? Have you any——' He stopped dead, and Helen breathed again as she saw some of the tension go out of him.

He was smiling in a self-derisive way again. 'I was about to ask whether you've any idea what I've been through since that day we had lunch together.'

Helen's smile was only a shadow of what she intended it to be. 'I have a vague idea.'

'And when you opened the door to me that day, I thought Corinne had been right all along. There was no light in your eyes. It was as though you couldn't care less about seeing me.'

Helen groaned audibly. 'Scot, I think that lunch date, that whole day, is best forgotten. I said . . . and did . . . Can we just say that that was my way of letting you go?'

Their eyes met in understanding and, this time, Scot's smile was real. 'And your date that night was to—to ease my conscience?'

Oh, but she was so relieved to see him smiling again! She tried to keep an impassive face, but her eyes lit up with mischief. 'Not at all! I did have a date. He was tall and dark and handsome.' She sighed, shrugging. 'But alas, he had a wife and four teenage sons.'

Scot grabbed hold of her wrist and pulled her towards him. 'Is that so? And how did you find that out?'

She looked at him blankly. 'When he brought them with him on our date, of course!'

He pulled her closer, locking her in the circle of his arms. 'Oh, Helen, my darling Helen, I'm too raw even to be kidded about your seeing another man!'

'Scot, listen to me.' She put her hands on either side of his face and looked into his eyes. 'What's done is done. Corinne failed. She *failed*. We're together now, and remember what they say about all being fair in love and war. She's to be pitied, Scot. She's in love with you, and pity is what I feel for her now. So don't be raw, and try not to be angry when love was her motive for. . . . What is it?'

Scot was looking at her as if he didn't know whether to laugh or to cry. '*Love?* Oh, Helen!' He put his hands on her shoulders and held her at arm's length, shaking her in the gentlest way. 'Trust you to think in those terms, the nicest terms! Bless your innocence, and may you stay as sweet at you are! The woman is not in love with me. Good God, not for one minute——'

'But she is. It's the wrong kind of love, a selfish kind, because she wouldn't be prepared to change her life for you in any way. But, as far as she's able and in her own fashion, she loves you.'

'Listen, darling one. Corinne married a man who was twenty-nine years her senior. Fine. And yes, she loved him in her fashion, she really did. But she told him quite plainly, as she told me at one time, that he had the necessary "qualifications" to be loved. He had money, bags of it. And she had none when she married him. He was also a surrogate father to her, and he was well aware of this, too. He told me so. He was to Corinne the father she'd never known, and that's why she genuinely loved him—in her fashion. She was unfaithful to him frequently, and he knew all about that, too.'

He went on patiently, 'Now then, as far as I'm concerned, she simply thinks she owns a piece of me. She thrives on the kind of life she leads in the States and——'

'I'm not sure that you're right. I accept all you've just said, but—well, she doesn't need you in order to stay in that kind of life. There are plenty of other people she can work for, if she insists on working. I wonder whether it's a combination of her loving you and——'

'Don't. Don't wonder any more. Just take my word for it.'

'But she *was kind* to me, when I met her. And she had no reason to be.'

'She *is* kind.' He smiled at Helen's confusion. 'She's an extraordinary character who's full of enigmas and contradictions. And she wasn't just pretending to like you later, either. She does. There was nothing personal in her trying to ruin your life. Corinne would give away the shirt off her back—but in business she will screw even the toughest of people into the ground in order to get an extra dollar. I know her, Helen, so don't wonder any more. She did all this to us because she thought she had a vested interest in me and my potential. Come to think of it, maybe she is a bit crazy.'

Helen was giving this serious thought until he put his hands around her waist. 'Forget Mrs Clayman. I don't want you to have anything else on your mind but me . . .'

She smiled at him as he pulled her closer, and Scot kissed her slowly but hungrily for a long, long time.

'What were we talking about?' she asked at length. 'I can't remember . . .'

He took hold of her left hand and led her to the settee. He kept hold of her hand as he reached for the velvet-covered box. 'Guesswork, Helen, I've no idea whether this will actually fit . . .'

The ring was just a little loose. She wiggled her fingers. 'Not bad for guesswork,' she smiled. 'It's a tiny bit loose.'

He covered the hand with his and held it tightly. 'We'll have it altered tomorrow, when we buy your wedding ring.'

She bobbed her head up and down, her eyes unusually bright as she looked at him.

Scot's eyes were filled with tenderness. 'Now go and pack your toothbrush. You're coming home with me for the night and——'

'Only for the night?' she giggled. 'What will your housekeeper think of that?'

'Nothing,' he smiled. 'Because you'll be sleeping in a guest room—such as it is at the moment.'

He stood up, and Helen laughed at him as he tapped himself on the ear. 'Just a minute, I don't think I heard myself correctly! I'm sure I just said you'll be sleeping in a guest room . . .' He pulled her to her feet, catching her tightly against him. 'Of course, you could always try persuading me to let you into my bed . . .'

Helen raised her brows, the blue depths of her eyes lit with happiness. 'Oh, I couldn't possibly do that! Not till we're married. I have my daughter's upbringing to consider!'

Just what the woman on the go needs!

BOOKMATE

The perfect "mate" for all Harlequin paperbacks!

Holds paperbacks open for hands-free reading!

- TRAVELING
- VACATIONING
- AT WORK • IN BED
- COOKING • EATING
- STUDYING

Perfect size for all standard paperbacks, this wonderful invention makes reading a pure pleasure! Ingenious design holds paperback books OPEN and FLAT so even wind can't ruffle pages—leaves your hands free to do other things. Reinforced, wipe-clean vinyl-covered holder flexes to let you turn pages without undoing the strap...supports paperbacks so well, they have the strength of hardcovers!

Snaps closed for easy carrying.

Available now. Send your name, address, and zip or postal code, along with a check or money order for just $4.99 + .75¢ for postage & handling (for a total of $5.74) payable to Harlequin Reader Service to:

Harlequin Reader Service

In the U.S.A.
2504 West Southern Ave.
Tempe, AZ 85282

In Canada
P.O. Box 2800, Postal Station A
5170 Yonge Street,
Willowdale, Ont. M2N 5T5

MATE-1R

Take these 4 best-selling novels FREE

Harlequin Presents

ANNE MATHER
born out of love

VIOLET WINSPEAR
time of the temptress

CHARLOTTE LAMB
man's world

SALLY WENTWORTH
say hello to yesterday

Take these 4 best-selling novels FREE

as advertised on TV

Yes! Four sophisticated, contemporary love stories by four world-famous authors of romance FREE, as your introduction to the Harlequin Presents subscription plan. Thrill to **Anne Mather**'s passionate story BORN OUT OF LOVE, set in the Caribbean.... Travel to darkest Africa in **Violet Winspear**'s TIME OF THE TEMPTRESS....Let **Charlotte Lamb** take you to the fascinating world of London's Fleet Street in MAN'S WORLD ....Discover beautiful Greece in **Sally Wentworth**'s moving romance SAY HELLO TO YESTERDAY.

Harlequin Presents...

The very finest in romance fiction

Join the millions of avid Harlequin readers all over the world who delight in the magic of a really exciting novel. EIGHT great NEW titles published EACH MONTH!
Each month you will get to know exciting, interesting, true-to-life people .... You'll be swept to distant lands you've dreamed of visiting .... Intrigue, adventure, romance, and the destiny of many lives will thrill you through each Harlequin Presents novel.

Get all the latest books before they're sold out!
As a Harlequin subscriber you actually receive your personal copies of the latest Presents novels immediately after they come off the press, so you're sure of getting all 8 each month.

Cancel your subscription whenever you wish!
You don't have to buy **any** minimum number of books. Whenever you decide to stop your subscription just let us know and we'll cancel all further shipments.

Your FREE gift includes

Anne Mather—Born out of Love
Violet Winspear—Time of the Temptress
Charlotte Lamb—Man's World
Sally Wentworth—Say Hello to Yesterday

FREE Gift Certificate
and subscription reservation

Mail this coupon today!

Harlequin Reader Service

In the U.S.A.
2504 West Southern Ave.
Tempe, AZ 85282

In Canada
P.O. Box 2800, Postal Station A
5170 Yonge Street,
Willowdale, Ont. M2N 5T5

Please send me my 4 Harlequin Presents books free. Also, reserve a subscription to the 8 new Harlequin Presents novels published each month. Each month I will receive 8 new Presents novels at the low price of $1.75 each [Total — $14.00 a month]. There are no shipping and handling or any other hidden charges. I am free to cancel at any time, but even if I do, these first 4 books are still mine to keep absolutely FREE without any obligation. **108 BPP CAEG**

NAME   (PLEASE PRINT)

ADDRESS   APT. NO.

CITY

STATE/PROV   ZIP/POSTAL CODE   P-SUB-3X

Offer expires December 31, 1984

If price changes are necessary you will be notified.

TAKE THESE 4 FREE

Harlequin Romances

as advertised on TV

Delight in **Mary Wibberley**'s warm romance, MAN OF POWER, the story of a girl whose life changes from drudgery to glamour overnight....Let THE WINDS OF WINTER by **Sandra Field** take you on a journey of love to Canada's beautiful Maritimes....Thrill to a cruise in the tropics—and a devastating love affair in the aftermath of a shipwreck— in **Rebecca Stratton**'s THE LEO MAN.... Travel to the wilds of Kenya in a quest for love with the determined heroine in **Karen van der Zee**'s LOVE BEYOND REASON.

Harlequin Romances . . . 6 exciting novels published each month! Each month you will get to know interesting, appealing, true-to-life people . . . . You'll be swept to distant lands you've dreamed of visiting . . . . Intrigue, adventure, romance, and the destiny of many lives will thrill you through each Harlequin Romance novel.

Get all the latest books before they're sold out!

As a Harlequin subscriber you actually receive your personal copies of the latest Romances immediately after they come off the press, so you're sure of getting all 6 each month.

Cancel your subscription whenever you wish!

You don't have to buy any minimum number of books. Whenever you decide to stop your subscription just let us know and we'll cancel all further shipments.

Your FREE gift includes

- MAN OF POWER by **Mary Wibberley**
- THE WINDS OF WINTER by **Sandra Field**
- THE LEO MAN by **Rebecca Stratton**
- LOVE BEYOND REASON by **Karen van der Zee**

FREE GIFT CERTIFICATE

and Subscription Reservation
Mail this coupon today!

Harlequin Reader Service

In the U.S.A.
2504 West Southern Ave.
Tempe, AZ 85282

In Canada
P.O. Box 2800, Postal Station A
5170 Yonge Street,
Willowdale, Ont. M2N 5T5

Please send me my 4 Harlequin Romance novels FREE. Also, reserve a subscription to the 6 NEW Harlequin Romance novels published each month. Each month I will receive 6 NEW Romance novels at the low price of $1.50 each (*Total–$9.00 a month*). There are no shipping and handling or any other hidden charges. I may cancel this arrangement at any time, but even if I do, these first 4 books are still mine to keep.   116 BPR EASU

NAME	(PLEASE PRINT)

ADDRESS	APT. NO.

CITY

STATE/PROV.	ZIP/POSTAL CODE

Offer not valid to present subscribers
Offer expires December 31, 1984   R-SUB-2X

If price changes are necessary you will be notified.

Harlequin Photo ～ Calendar ～

Turn Your Favorite Photo into a Calendar.

JULY 1984

The Browns

Uniquely yours, this 10x17½" calendar features your favorite photograph, with any name you wish in attractive lettering at the bottom. A delightfully personal and practical idea!

Send us your favorite color print, black-and-white print, negative, or slide, any size (we'll return it), along with **3** proofs of purchase (coupon below) from a June or July release of Harlequin Romance, Harlequin Presents, Harlequin Superromance, Harlequin American Romance or Harlequin Temptation, plus $5.75 (includes shipping and handling).

Harlequin Photo Calendar Offer
(PROOF OF PURCHASE)

NAME_____
(Please Print)

ADDRESS_____

CITY_____ STATE_____ ZIP_____

NAME ON CALENDAR_____

Mail photo, 3 proofs,
plus check or money order
for $5.75 payable to:

Harlequin Books
P.O. Box 52020
Phoenix, AZ 85072

2-6

Expires December 31, 1984. (Not available in Canada)

CAL-1